PUSHKIN PRESS

HIROMI KAWAKAMI was born in Tokyo in 1958. She has written numerous novels—among them *Strange Weather in Tokyo*, *The Nakano Thrift Shop* and *Manazuru*—and short-story collections, and has garnered many of Japan's top literary prizes. Kawakami was shortlisted for both the 2013 Man Asian Literary Prize, and the 2014 *Independent* Foreign Fiction Prize. Her work has been published in more than twenty languages. Her story "A Snake Stepped On" in this collection won the prestigious Akutagawa Prize in 1996.

LUCY NORTH, born in Kuala Lumpur, Malaysia, studied at the University of Cambridge and Harvard University and has a PhD in modern Japanese literature. Her translations of Taeko Kōno were published in *Toddler Hunting and Other Stories*. Lucy lived for many years in Boston and Tokyo, and is now based in Hastings, on the south coast of England.

HIROMI KAWAKAMI

RECORD

of a

NIGHT
TOO BRIEF

translated by
LUCY NORTH

PUSHKIN PRESS

SERIES EDITORS: David Karashima and Michael Emmerich

TRANSLATION EDITOR: Elmer Luke

Pushkin Press

71–75 Shelton Street

London, WC2H 9JQ

HEBI O FUMU © Hiromi Kawakami, 1996

English language translation © Lucy North 2017

Record of a Night Too Brief was first published as *Hebi o Fumu* in 1996

First published by Pushkin Press in 2017

Parts of "Record of a Night Too Brief" appeared, in slightly
different form, in *Words without Borders*, July 2012.

The publisher gratefully acknowledges the support of the
British Centre for Literary Translation and the Nippon Foundation

5 7 9 8 6 4

ISBN 9781782272717

Designed and typeset in Marbach by Tetragon, London
Printed by CPI Group (UK) Ltd, Croydon, CR0 4YY

www.pushkinpress.com

CONTENTS

RECORD OF A NIGHT TOO BRIEF

1 HORSE

What was that itch on my back? I wondered. And then I realized that it was the night—the night was nibbling into me.

It wasn't that late, still only twilight, but the darkness seemed to have collected just above my shoulders. A black clump of it had fastened onto me, eating away at my back.

I wriggled, trying to shake it off, but the night clung fast. When I tried to rip it off with my hands, it floated away, as vapour, and I couldn't grasp it. I grabbed at a patch, where it was most intensely black, but immediately it dispersed, and another black patch swirled up somewhere else.

The itchiness became unbearable. I scratched frantically. The more I scratched, the more the darkness ate into my back, and the more the darkness ate into my back, the more I itched.

Unable to stand still, I broke into a run.

Immediately, I was running as fast as a horse. I thought, as I ran: you get faster when the night starts eating into you. Roads, pedestrians, signs, all fly by, retreating into the distance, like scenes through a train window.

After a minute or two I grew sick of running, so I stopped. My body was giving off steam like a horse. I was breathing loudly through my nose. Some of the darkness merged with the steam, producing swirling, hazy eddies.

People, standing at a distance, stared.

The darkness mixed with the breaths I was taking in, reappearing when I breathed out, floating in long trails. When I inhaled, the dark trails near my nostrils were sucked back in. When I exhaled again, they were longer than before. The darkness grew, stretching out like endless ribbons, issuing forth from my nostrils.

"That's a sight you don't see every day," an onlooker exclaimed, and then clapped, purposefully, as if summoning koi to the surface of a pond. The other onlookers clapped too, in just the same way.

I grew irritated. "Get the fuck outta here!" I tried to shout.

But no words emerged from my mouth. I couldn't get the first consonant out. Straining, blowing through my nostrils, bearing down, I tried for that first sound: "G— G— G—" But all I could manage was to snort and blow out air.

The onlookers were delighted, and clapped some more.

This infuriated me. I leapt into the air, trying to yell at them, but all that came out was a whinny—like I was a horse. I kept leaping. Landing on a roof, I whinnied again—and then again. The onlookers below were all clapping. I wasn't going to be outdone by them, and I kept whinnying. By now I had acquired a horse's body, and was covered with a thick black coat of hair.

"Night's coming. The Night Horse has arrived," an onlooker said—the first in the crowd to have clapped. At that moment the steam started to rise in clouds off my body. More darkness: spreading, covering everything.

Elated now, I whinnied over and over again. With every whinny, the darkness became blacker and more intense.

2 CHAOS

While I was walking, the number of people increased. We were all going in the same direction. I walked, swept along in the flow.

It was after dusk, an hour closer to night. I could see the outlines of people walking just ahead of me, but couldn't tell the colour of their clothes. A lamplighter approached, holding a long pole, pushing his way against the stream of people. Raising the pole up to a lamp, he let it rest there a few seconds, and the lamp started to glow. Looking around, I realized that there were several lamplighters: everywhere about me, one street lamp after another started to give out a steady light.

Now there were even more people walking, and it was difficult keeping up the pace.

"Are you going too?"

I glanced over my shoulder, and saw a slender girl with short hair walking behind me.

"I was thinking about it...," I answered, without quite committing myself.

Hearing this, the girl, who didn't stop walking, removed an envelope from her satchel, and opened it, all the while keeping pace with the stream of people.

In the envelope were some green tickets.

"I have an extra. You take it," she said, as she quickly slipped the green ticket into my pocket. I was going to thank her—but she waved me off and pointed at the people behind us. Some kind of hitch had stopped the flow of people, and there was a pile-up. Knots of people were starting to form, and as more people kept coming from behind them, soon some of the knots were getting pushed up into the air, on top of the knots of people below them.

Quickly I turned to face forward again, and started to walk. A long gap had opened up between us and the people in front of us. Thinking I ought to catch up with them, I broke into a run. But again the girl stopped me.

"Don't run, or we'll have chaos. It's too early. Too early."

I didn't understand what she was referring to, but in any case I resumed walking.

We seemed to be approaching a termination point. The stream of people was spreading out. Just ahead, something very tall was rising up to the sky.

Several dozen ticket collectors stood in a row, and once we passed through, showing our tickets, the tall object came into better view.

It was a singer, who stood as tall as a three-storey building. From where I was, I had a clear view of the beauty spot under her jaw, and the rise and fall of her breasts.

"The beauty spot is artificial," the girl informed me, gazing up at the singer, enraptured.

The singer was producing notes at different pitches, as if she were warming up. When she sang high notes, flocks of birds took flight from the branches of the gingko trees. When she sang low notes, the earth heaved, and small furry creatures emerged from underground and crawled about.

When the square was packed with people, suddenly, with no warning, the singer commenced singing. It was as if an immense musical instrument was filling the firmament with sound, or as if the melody of her song was swimming through the skies... In the next moment her voice had overwhelmed all else, and rather than listening, we seemed to be encompassed within it. No longer able to know the words, we were conscious only that her lilting voice was, slowly and powerfully, all around us.

The crowd of people, filled with her music, started to break up and form lines, which began to flow from the square in every direction, like innumerable streams flowing from a lake.

"The chaos has started," the girl said to me, joining a stream of people going by her. I watched as she was borne away.

I joined the same stream of people, and pretty soon caught up with her.

"Where are we going?" I enquired. The girl nodded several times, her eyes closed, looking unworried.

"Where?" I asked again.

"The night," she replied.

With that, her head tilted downwards, and she fell into a deep sleep. She was carried along as she slept.

Now a part of the chaos, alongside the girl, I entered the night.

3 GENTLEMEN

I ascended the stairs and found a door, which I opened to a banquet in full swing.

An array of gentlemen, each of them dressed in white, was seated at a table, eating and drinking. On the table were platters of raw seafood—sea urchin, halibut, scallops, clams, sea bream, flounder, silver trevally, tuna, squid, octopus, smelt—as well as an assortment of meat and vegetable dishes—broiled, boiled, fried. The gentlemen were savouring each dish.

I could hear them having little disagreements, in the soft-spoken manner befitting gentlemen.

"This part, just here. *So* succulent! Such *flavour*!"

"Oh, but it shouldn't be soft. When it's utterly fresh, it's springy and firm. That's the whole point."

"So the divers have to gather it up from the seabed in the early hours."

"That's what makes it such a luxury."

The food looked so mouth-wateringly delicious, I swallowed loudly, despite myself.

The gentlemen, unaware of my presence, turned and trained their gaze on me.

"Who do we have here? A traveller, perhaps, from a distant land?"

"A visitor."

"We don't often get visitors."

"We should mark the occasion!"

They all rose from the table. The gentleman at the head placed his napkin on his chair and approached me, his arms open.

"So good of you to come!" he said.

And the others, who'd followed his lead placing their napkins on their chairs and greeting me, added their chorus of welcomes.

I was shown to a seat midway along the table, a napkin was tucked in at my collar, and a gleaming knife and fork placed beside me.

"Please, eat."

"Please feel free, have whatever you like."

The gentlemen took their seats at the table. The gentlemen

on my right turned to the left, and the gentlemen on my left turned to the right. Two lines of faces, on both sides of the table, their eyes all fixed on the same point, receded into the distance on either side of me, like two lines of layered images.

"Please try the flounder. It's out of this world."

"And the cooked dishes—the stir-fried chicken with chilli peppers."

"Or the pig's liver *gayettes*."

"If you'd prefer a dish with green curry, we'll have it prepared specially."

With all this encouragement, I was unable to decide. My fork hovered over the dishes. The gentlemen fixed their gaze, their eyes wide, on the end of my fork. They seemed almost to be drooling.

I stuck the fork into something that looked like meat, I wasn't sure what kind, on a plate near me.

A sigh rose up from the company.

"Ahh!"

"Would you expect less from a guest from a distant land?"

"Such a discriminating palate!"

I cut the meat, or whatever it was, and ate it, piece by tiny piece. But I couldn't taste it.

"What'll she go for now, I wonder?"

"Come now, no more comments. Leave her to enjoy it."

I continued to eat. With every bite, sighs and cries of joy and muffled surprise rose up, and I became even less able to taste what I was eating.

I had now eaten my fill, so I laid down my knife and fork. But the gentlemen glared at me.

"Our guest eats surprisingly little."

"She's probably just having a rest."

"She couldn't possibly want to stop eating yet."

Embarrassed, I resumed eating. My stomach was so full I thought it might burst, but still I ate. I ate till nearly everything on the table was gone. I sighed in relief, thinking I was done, when one of the gentlemen rang a bell, which made a little tinkling sound.

A butler appeared, bringing out platters with dome-like silver dish covers.

"Our guest is fortunate!"

"Fortunate to be able to enjoy such a rare feast!"

"She can eat her fill, whatever she likes, until dawn breaks!"

I really felt that I could not force down another morsel. But the gentlemen were all staring at me sternly, even as they smiled.

Outside a nightingale started to sing in a high voice.

Please, I can't eat anything more, I wanted to say, but I couldn't.

The nightingale sang again. The plates on the table gleamed, and the food, in all its ceaseless variety, breathed, glossy and bright.

The night had only just begun.

4 THE BIG CRUNCH

I assumed that we'd been borne along for a while, but when I awoke, time was at a standstill. Since time had stopped, even if we had been moving for a while, no actual hours, or moments, would have passed.

The hair of the girl who had been carried along with me had grown down to her hips. So even if time had stood still, her hair had grown.

Good morning, I said, seeing she was awake. She laughed softly. It's too early to say that, she said. It's still evening. And she smiled.

Really? It's evening now?

The girl entwined her arms with mine.

Some of her long hair got entwined as well. It felt silky and warm.

Your hair has grown, I said.

Yours hasn't though, she replied.

It was true. My hair hadn't grown an inch.

The girl's hair rose, like a living being, and stroked my neck and shoulders. When I brought my face near hers, the girl exhaled gently out of her slightly opened mouth. The scent of her breath was like the odour of lilies at full bloom, and the sound of her breath coming out of her mouth was like a butterfly faintly beating its wings.

I kissed the girl on the lips, as if to suck her breath inside me. When I did this, the girl wilted, ever so slightly. In my arms, gradually she became lighter, and more transparent. The smell of lilies rose up, filling my breast, overwhelming me. The taste of the kiss was so sweet, I couldn't stop—even though I knew she would go on wilting if I continued. The girl was wilting by the instant, and something thick and strong was filling my breast.

Holding the girl in the palm of my hand, for by now she had shrunk so that it was possible to do so, I continued to kiss her. A numbness came over me, covering me from the top of my head to the tips of my toes: I felt as if I was now enfolded by something soft and huge. Revelling in the sensation of being wrapped in giant overlapping petals, I kept my lips placed on the lips of the girl, who was now getting quite crumpled and tiny.

The girl finally grew incredibly small, about one centimetre wide. I no longer knew whether I was kissing her or simply enjoying the afterglow of the kiss, but now the girl's breath was filled with the overpowering scent of lilies, and the sound of her breathing, like the beating of butterfly wings, grew loud, almost annoyingly loud.

As I looked at the girl in the palm of my hand, she shone whitely in the night. When I stroked her gently, she seemed beautifully lustrous, and I was struck by how smooth she was, by how she was warm but cold at the same time, and then, looking more closely, I realized she had become a pearl. In the depths of the pearl, I could see the girl's face staring back at me, and, if I peered into the depths of her eyes, I could see another, smaller girl.

An endless number of girls, getting infinitely smaller and smaller, and all emitting the same scented breath, were quietly but persistently enticing me to go further. When I rolled the pearl over my palm, exploring its smooth surface, they all laughed gently, flutteringly, in response, drawing me in even more.

I put the pearl in my mouth, let it rest on my tongue for a while, and swallowed it.

The infinite number of girls descended my throat, passed down into my stomach, and were transmitted through my veins to all parts of my body. Waves of explosive pleasure rushed over me. Then I realized: my hair had started to grow. And time, previously at a standstill, had started to flow again.

Time continued to flow, as the granules of girl reached every nook and cranny of me. The girl was broken down into something very tiny indeed, tinier even than the smallest particle, and still she coursed round and round. The girl became more and more mixed and homogeneous with me, until in the end I lost track of whether the girl was me, or I was the girl. It was only then that I started to love her, and to miss her. I loved and missed something I couldn't define, some combination of us both.

At this thought, time came to a standstill. A little while later, I was assailed by contractions of unbelievable force.

5 JAPANESE MACAQUE

No matter how much I poured into the cup, it never filled. And then I realized that the liquid I assumed to be coffee had, unbeknownst to me, turned into night.

Peering into the night as it poured into the cup, I could see tiny stars and gases whirling near the surface, and down at the bottom, something laughing. In dismay, I took the cup to a sink, and tipped it so that all the night it contained would spill out, but as long as I held it there, the night kept on flowing, interminably.

I had been holding the cup there for a good hour, and still the night came. No matter how much was sucked away down the drain, there was always more. Resigning myself, I turned the cup upright and peered into it again: at this the laughter coming up from the bottom of the cup grew very loud. I hurled the cup against the wall. From the broken shards the soft clouds of night floated up, spreading outwards. And there, in among them, was the laughter's source.

It was a large Japanese macaque.

It was laughing loudly, baring its teeth, exposing its gums. I was surprised that a monkey was laughing just like a human being: so I gave it a poke with the end of a mop to see what it would do.

At this, the monkey abruptly stopped laughing.

"Do you *have* to be so rude?" it demanded, in a terrifying voice.

I tried to apologize but my tongue seemed to stick to my palate, and no sound came out.

"Didn't your parents teach you *any* manners at *all*?" the monkey shouted at me, even more loudly.

I made several small bows, and shuffled back bit by bit. The monkey edged forward.

"Apologize!" it bellowed. Its voice was ear-splittingly loud—the vibrations produced cracks in the room's walls.

I shuffled back some more, and the monkey again roared, "Apologize!" At this, the entire ceiling came crashing down.

In the nick of time I opened the door and rushed into the corridor, and out into the night. Several neighbours had come out of their houses: they were pointing at the collapsed ceiling and talking among themselves. I ran off, pushing my way through them. When an angry monkey, howling at the top of his lungs, appeared from the rubble, the staring onlookers scattered in all directions, like baby spiders.

Blind with rage, the monkey swatted away several people who had been slow on the uptake, sending them flying into the distance. Turning back, I caught sight of them disappearing into the night, tracing parabolic curves, whooping and laughing as they went. For a moment, fascinated, I was about to stop, but then I realized that the monkey was just behind me, breathing roughly, and so I started running again.

"Apologize!" the monkey said, panting for breath.

I wanted to apologize but the momentum was taking my legs forward. They wouldn't stop.

"Apologize!" Soon the monkey's panting turned to wheezing, and inside the wheezing, another sound could be heard, something rather like thunder.

"Apologize!" the monkey said, close to the back of my neck. And immediately twenty or more rumbles of thunder boomed about us. The rumbles gradually got louder and louder, and flashes of lightning lit up the sky. The intervals between them shortened, and soon the crashes of thunder and flashes of lightning were occurring simultaneously. Several times a bolt of lightning struck something, and the surrounding darkness was lit up dazzlingly, then went black again. The speed with which my feet hit the ground got faster with each crash.

I appeared to be running faster than the speed of sound because suddenly there was no longer any thunder to be heard. I could only see flashes of lightning, which continued unceasingly, and inside them the silhouette of the monkey as it charged along after me. I couldn't hear its commands to "Apologize!" any more. I continued to run, with all my might, through the soundless void.

Soon, exhaustion overcame me, my legs began to feel heavy, and the monkey caught up. It didn't slow down. In an instant it had passed me, and no sooner had it gone by than it disappeared.

Little by little, my pace slowed and I began to hear sounds again—the heavy breathing of the monkey, peals of thunder—muted at first, like sounds heard underwater, but gradually getting clearer. The next instant, they all joined together in a great cacophony, which pressed in on me and burst.

Within the sudden inundation of sound, at the very bottom of it, was a sound much louder than anything else. I listened to it and realized it was laughter.

It was that same monkey's laughter, noticeably more powerful and more resonant than any of the other many noises that were echoing in the night.

6 DECIMATION

My mass had been missing for a while. You tend to assume that without any mass you wouldn't exist. But I was definitely there. Hard to believe, but it was true.

Not only was I there, the girl was there with me, right by my side. She didn't have any mass either. I knew she was there because I could hear her moving about in places where nothing could be seen.

I was just about to call out to her when our surroundings were suddenly illuminated by a blaze of light.

The light was shining out of a corner of the night sky. In just that part, a bit of the sky seemed to have been cut out and the night peeled back into a square, so that the light streamed through the square hole, straight down to the ground, in a single shaft. To a bystander, it would probably have looked as if a square-shaped pillar of light was rising straight up out of the ground towards the heavens.

Bathed in that light, we found we did have mass after all. The light was a special, miraculous kind. But as we had only a tiny amount of mass, we were both extremely small—smaller, even, than mice.

Small as I was, I turned to the girl, and told her: "I love you." With the light pouring down, I repeated the words several times. And each time I said them, a curious creature emerged out of the earth.

The first creature to emerge seemed to be a failed version of the girl. She was about twice the size of the small girl by my side, and made of metal. Creaking, she made her way out of the shaft of light.

The second creature was another failed version of the girl. This one was silver. I thought at first she looked silver because of the silvery light, but even when she walked out of it she still shone with a silvery lustre. Her face, her hands, and her legs—every part of her glittered, menacingly. The silver girl followed in the footsteps of the metal girl. The glow of her silvery image lingered in my eye.

The third creature was yet another failed version of the girl. This one was almost identical to her in every way; the only thing different was that she had a tail. After wagging her tail wildly for a while, she hurried off after the first two versions.

I was about to say "I love you" a fourth time when the girl put out her hand and stopped my mouth, gently. Her hand as she touched my lips smelt of the night. I didn't want it there, and grasping her wrist gently, I moved it away.

"Why?" I asked.

"You know why. Because it's a lie," she replied.

I hugged her gently, and she hugged me back, equally gently.

"It's not something you say so easily," she said as she hugged me.

She's right, I thought, as we hugged each other, but before very long I wanted to tell her I loved her again.

Well, why don't we stop, then, if it's a lie! I blurted out.

As soon as I spoke, the ground started to roar and rumble, and in the next second it split open. Two more beings emerged—myself and the girl, this time perfectly accurately massed. To us, these two beings seemed gigantic: smiling benignly, using their gigantic eyes, they had no difficulty in locating the first girl, the imperfect metal one; and the second girl, the imperfect silver one; and the third girl, the one that had a tail, in the darkness. They shut them away in a briefcase. Then, turning towards us, they plucked up my companion, and locked her in there too.

Are they going to lock *me* up now? I wondered. And before I knew it, they had.

That was it: I was locked up, for ever.

7 LOACHES

There were a number of fish in the tank. They looked like loaches. Someone was scooping them up, one by one, with his hands and throwing them down hard on the floor.

It was a child.

Once thrown down, the loach lay in a half-dead state for a few seconds, then revived and shimmied its way over to one of the many puddles nearby, leaving arteries of water on the floor behind it.

"If you throw them down so hard, the loaches will die," I said, reprovingly.

The child frowned. "They won't die," he replied in a low voice, and continued throwing them down—*thwack! thwack!*—on the floor.

He had been scooping up the loaches and throwing them down for quite some time, but it didn't seem to make a difference to the number of fish in the tank. A small fluorescent light had been attached to it, illuminating it against the darkness. The child was standing slightly out of reach of the glow, so I couldn't make out the features of his face.

He continued throwing the loaches down, one after another. But far from decreasing, the number of loaches in the tank seemed to be increasing.

"Do you like Yanagawa hotpot?" the child asked.

"What?" I said.

"Yanagawa loach hotpot," the child repeated, throwing down another loach with force. *Thwack.*

"I don't mind it."

"In that case, I'll give you this fish tank." His voice had got lower.

Why hadn't I walked past him and paid no attention to the loaches?

The child pulled at my sleeve with a wet hand, slipping a loach into my hand. "Try one!" he said, throwing down another loach.

At the bottom of the darkness, near my feet, I could see loaches making their way, shimmying, towards the puddles. As they slipped below the surface, the water seemed to vanish, then slowly to reappear.

"No. I can do without loaches," I replied.

The child's head drooped. "Are you sure?" he asked, and then he started to whimper.

I got a strong sense of foreboding at this, and I decided I'd better get away from him. Furtively putting the loach he'd deposited in my hand down on the floor, I began to walk away with an unconcerned look on my face. But the second I had put the loach down, a big puddle had formed in that very spot, spreading to my feet. The puddle looked like an oil spill, very thick and sticky: when the loaches found their way into it, it swallowed them up, without a ripple.

"Are you sure?" the child asked again.

"Quite sure!" I replied.

At that, the child shoved me, and I fell into a puddle. I found myself being sucked into it. When I was completely submerged, I looked around me. Everything was dark. Was it dark because it was night, or because the puddle was filled with black creatures? I wasn't sure, but as my eyes got used to the darkness, I could see.

Down below, at the bottom of the puddle, where I was now sinking, I could see countless loaches. *No way... No way!* I thought, and looking at my hands I saw that they were turning into fins—and my legs merging into a tail. I concentrated on my repugnance for loaches, and my fins started turning back into hands, but when my concentration waned, they immediately started turning back into fins.

"Are you so sure you don't want the fish tank?"

The low voice of the child reached my ears from above.

The words stuck in my throat, but I knew I had no choice.

"I *love* Yanagawa hotpot!" I shouted up at him.

Suddenly I found myself scooped up in the child's hands, and thrown down hard against the floor. I wriggled my way towards the child's feet, and then shimmied up one of his legs. I kept going up to his hips, and from his hips to his belly, and finally I reached an arm. I then wriggled down this arm to his fingers, at which point he grabbed hold of me, and threw me down to the floor.

Seven times we repeated the process, until eventually I turned back into a human.

"You really love Yanagawa hotpot, don't you," the child said, laying it on thick.

"Oh yes, I *love* Yanagawa hotpot!" I replied, again.

After pressing the tank into my hands, the child flopped-flipped-flopped in a puddle, then disappeared. The puddle was still, and then it too disappeared.

The loaches in the tank were multiplying rapidly. The tank teemed with loaches.

I hurried home, careful not to let any water spill into the night, and began preparations for a loach hotpot. I sliced up burdock root, added water, and brought it all to a boil, using all the stewing pots I had. Then I threw the loaches live into the pots, and covered them. A delicious aroma rose into the air.

"You really can't get enough of Yanagawa hotpot, can you?" I heard a child's voice say from somewhere, one more time. As if in response, all the creatures that live and breathe in the night made their way into my apartment through the crack in my door. And they all had a Yanagawa hotpot feast.

8 SCHRÖDINGER'S CAT

Without my noticing, the girl and I had become separated. I looked for her everywhere, but could not find her.

The moon had risen to the highest place in the sky, and on the ground the shadows of the plants were dimly lit in the faint moonlight.

"Where are you? Where are you?" I called out, but there was no answer from the girl. I called out many times, but she did not answer.

As I walked, following one shimmering shape in the moonlight to the next, I found several of the girl's soft outer skins that she must have discarded. Each time I saw one, I would gather it up in my hands, thinking it was the real girl, but every discarded skin was simply a discarded skin.

I didn't know why I was searching so hard for the girl: I felt she was someone I had known all my life, and yet at the same time I hardly knew her. But I kept on looking. If someone had asked me if I liked her, I would probably have answered, yes, I did, but if someone had asked me whether I really cared about her, I might have answered, no, I didn't, actually. Maybe the only reason I kept searching for her was that I had begun searching for her.

The discarded skin I now picked up was the largest yet, and it was still a bit warm. She was probably hiding somewhere nearby. I walked on, calling out, "Where are you? Where are you?"

At a spot where the shadows outlined by the moon abruptly stopped, there was a big box. I reached out to touch it, and felt it tremble.

The girl must be inside the box, I felt sure. In front of the box was a discarded skin even larger than the one I had found a moment ago. It was lying on the ground, looking just like the living girl with her knees slightly bent. I stroked it gently. But being only a skin, it didn't have the slightest response.

I searched for a latch, some way to open the box, but it was just a smooth white box, nothing more. I sat there, wondering what to do, when the box trembled some more.

Open me up! it seemed to be saying. Or maybe it was saying: *Don't open me!* Again, it shook. I clasped the box in my arms, and rubbed my cheek against it.

Simply doing this, of course, was going to get me nowhere. Somehow I had to force the box open. But the surface was completely smooth, sealed. I tried poking at the box with a pocket knife, but the blade simply bounced off the surface.

I walked back and forth, thinking.

Again the box trembled. I wondered: should I get an axe and chop it open? But that might end up splitting the girl in half. Well, maybe I should take the box home with me, just as it was, to stroke and treat it with affection for all eternity. But that would be no different from being without the girl altogether.

I thought on and on.

How would one describe the girl now, as she was inside the box? It was like she was there, only she wasn't; or like she wasn't, except that she was. Or maybe she occupied an indeterminate state of being, both there and not there, in exactly equal amounts.

I thought and thought, nudging the outer skin on the ground with the tip of my foot.

I thought until, unable to stand it any more, I rushed home, grabbed a sledgehammer, retraced my steps, and smashed the box open.

There, in the shattered box, lay the girl. As I had feared, she was in pieces, completely destroyed. Heartbroken, I started to sob. Why did I smash the box? I thought bitterly. But how could I have stopped myself?

How could anyone endure such a state, of having someone there and not there—not there and there—at the same time?

Deeply indignant at this quandary of quantum physics, I cried and cried.

9 MOLE

As I collided with the man, several moles fell out of the front of his jacket.

"Oh, bother! Bother!" the man said, desperately trying to rake them together with his hands.

I walked on by, pretending I hadn't noticed. Nothing good ever comes of getting caught up with people you meet in the night.

"Hey, wait! Wait!" the man yelled.

He appeared to be chasing the moles, going round in circles, but I didn't look back and walked off as quickly as I could.

I walked just until he was out of earshot, and then I stopped. He did not appear to be following me. I waited a while, but there was not a single sign of him. I waited a few more minutes. Not the slightest sound. I could see the moon, high up in the sky, and I could feel the breeze gently caressing my skin, but nothing of what I was expecting might happen was happening.

Disappointed, I retraced my steps.

But, as the saying goes, seek too keenly, and ye shall never find. Sure enough, as far back along the path as I went, I could find no trace of him. Occasionally, though, I would catch sight of the odd mole dawdling about, so I continued back along the path, using these sightings as beacons.

I must have walked on a bit too single-mindedly, for the next thing I knew, I was on a path that seemed unfamiliar. There came a slow, lilting melody. I listened to its strains, and felt drowsy. I won't listen, I won't listen, I told myself, but the music seemed to pour into my ears of its own accord, producing a feeling now of utter physical and spiritual tranquillity.

In that state, I stretched myself out on the path. I could detect a faint warmth in the earth, left over from the day. Ah, I'm falling asleep, I thought. But the next moment, I was being rudely roused by the man.

"*You transverse piece of lowlife!*" he yelled.

I leapt to my feet.

"You think you can get away with such *lopsided logic?*"

Astounded, I stared at him.

The insults continued.

"*Don't you have any triangular consciousness at all?*"

"You're *a pest!* A *quadri-transmogrifying pest!*"

"I've a good mind to break you, fold you, then turn you upside-down and shake you. Then *drop you in a pot!*"

I was so blown back by the force of his words I couldn't reply, but then he stopped abruptly. Looking closely at him, I saw his face resembled a mole's. Actually, "resembled" was not the word: *he was a mole.* Struggling to conceal the moles packed down his jacket, Moley-Man resumed his invective.

"Two days ago, it would have been the *Great Depression* for *you*, oh yes, that's for sure!"

"And a *ding-dong, sing-song, plinkety-plunk: You better watch out! Hey Hey Hey... Pop!*"

This was all getting difficult to make sense of. Oh well, he was a mole—what could I expect? I decided to keep silent and wait for him to finish. Evidently thinking me intimidated, he gradually got calmer. Finally, he just stood there, breathing short quick breaths.

He came up to me, now panting heavily.

I looked up in fright, and saw he was just about to put his hands on my shoulders. He brought his snout close to my face, sniffing and snuffling, with little whiny sounds. He sniffed again, carefully. When he had sniffed his fill, his expression suddenly softened:

"Well, *hello!*" Then: "That was a little rude of me. Heh, heh! Do excuse me. Got a little on edge for a moment there..."

He seemed to have made a complete U-turn.

"Come now. Let's be friends," he said.

He put out a paw. The back of it was as black as coal, and he had long, strong claws. I shook it, and stole a glance, and saw he was blinking repeatedly, nervously.

I told myself firmly: Do not let down your guard.

"Do you have any hobbies?"

"How's business these days?"

"Do you know any nice cafes round here?"

His questions came thick and fast. Answering in what I hoped was the least objectionable way possible, I stole more glances, trying to suss out the situation.

Without intending to be, we were back on the familiar path: I could hear the strains of that same melody. I told myself to keep my wits about me, but when that tune found its way into my ears, something inside me fell apart.

By the time he asked me, "What do you feel is the most important quality in a man?" I was filled with a feeling of such recklessness, I was ready to throw caution to the winds. My mouth was itching to say it.

I said it in a low voice.

He didn't appear to have heard me. "What's that?" he asked, loudly.

"That he's loaded. Loaded with moles..."

As soon as I uttered the words, the moles stuffed down his jacket burst out, tumbling onto the path.

The man clutched his fists.

"Loaded with moles?..." He was shaking all over.

The moles poured forth in a continuous stream, falling on top of each other at our feet. The ground was teeming with them. The moles filled the night with their eloquent, scrabbling sounds.

10 CLONING

For a while, I just cried, as I gathered together the bits of the girl. But since nothing would be accomplished by crying, I decided I would take the bits to the Boss.

As I got closer to the Boss, I could hear a steady, continuous noise, which got louder and louder. It was a huge windmill, whose blades were going round and round, whirring. The windmill was located behind the throne where the Boss sat. It was pulling in the night, stirring it around.

Sucked in and turned around by the blades, the night at first flows smoothly, but then it starts to take on a denser consistency. Already the night was nearly halfway through its course, so a good portion of it had hardened. Because of this, as I walked through it, it gave me none of the easy, buoyant feeling you get in the early-evening hours. Something about it seemed creaky. But that was, in its own way, typical of the night too.

"I'd like to request a replay," I said, dropping to the ground on my knees and bowing my head low.

"A replay, you say?" the Boss replied, narrowing his eyes.

The Boss's body sank low in the throne. He was not a very big Boss. The enormous blue jewel in the sceptre he was holding sparkled brightly.

"It is my humble understanding that the Boss possesses the power to bring about a replay, and that is why..." I bowed again, very low, head to the ground.

But before I could raise my head, he growled:

"Request refused."

"What?"

"Why would I want to do that, for a *girl*!"

And he refused to engage any more. I tried my most obsequious bow a number of times. To no avail. Maybe he didn't really enjoy all this formalized ceremony.

I got up and was about to go on my way when something tapped me on the shoulder. It felt hard; I realized it was the tip of the sceptre.

"*I* won't do it, but if you insist, you may have a try yourself," he said, now poking me with the sceptre.

As I stood there in a quandary, he poked me again, several times. With each poke, the enormous blue jewel in the sceptre sparkled.

"Thank you," I answered, finding this unbearable.

He finally stopped poking me and sank back down in his throne. The windmill made its loud whirring sound.

I walked to a place that was a distance away from the Boss, and then divided the bits of the girl into piles, carefully extracting the cell nuclei that looked as if they could be used for the replay. Copying the Boss's usual practice, I injected a small amount of cell nuclei into the inside of my elbow with a micropipette, and then, again copying the Boss's usual practice, I turned three somersaults. I had no idea how a somersault would help with a replay, but I wanted to do everything the exact same way the Boss did, so that's what I did.

I waited a few moments, and then I dozed off.

I snoozed for a while, and woke up to find it was still night. So that meant there had been no replay, I thought, disappointed, but then, examining the inner part of my elbow, lo and behold, there were some new cells!

Overjoyed, I pressed my back against the ground, and spun myself round and round like a top. It was part of a little dance. I didn't know what this was supposed to accomplish, but here again I was copying the Boss. The cells were gradually forming themselves into shapes—commas, ribbons, balls, all sorts of other weird things—and finally they turned into something that resembled a girl. By now my arm was getting numb with the weight of this girl-like thing. The time had come for separation, I understood, so I tied her stalk up with wire. Immediately, her stalk rotted, and she dropped off me.

She immediately did the replay dance, and then came and gave me a kiss.

The girl had come back to life. But she seemed mechanical, so I wasn't totally convinced. I didn't return her kiss very enthusiastically. She didn't seem to care, and kissed me again.

The whirring sound of the windmill could be heard from far away. Coagulated bits of the night air were flung against me, and then unstuck themselves and flew off in great lumps somewhere else.

"You don't care about me any more, do you?" the girl said, sensing my lack of enthusiasm.

"It's not that," I answered, vaguely.

The girl threw herself on the ground, wailing.

I was determined not to care.

"Why did you revive me then? Why did you bother?" she said, and started to sob loudly.

This irritated me, so I turned my back on her and started to walk away. The girl clung to me, crying.

"That's so mean of you. To bring things this far..."

Nothing she said had the slightest effect on me. I knew I was being heartless, but it couldn't be helped.

"Please. Please reconsider," the girl begged.

The bits of coagulated night were now hitting me with more force, then falling about me like a meteor shower. I shook my head, dodging the paths of the flying lumps.

"All right, so that's what you want. But I have my own ideas."

There was a flash of silver, and the girl lunged at me with a knife, wielding it wildly.

Before I had time to react, the girl cut a piece of flesh from my right breast, then turned and raced away. I looked, dazed, at the blood dripping, and with a start it came to me what she was up to.

I made my way stealthily back, without being seen, to the place where the Boss was. As I thought, the girl was just handing the Boss the bit of flesh. The Boss nodded magnanimously, and immediately carried out a replay. As I watched, an exact replica of myself was born. The girl received the replica with an air of satisfaction.

After watching the girl leave hand-in-hand with the replica, I presented myself before the Boss.

"Is this how it's supposed to go?" I asked.

The Boss cleared his throat, and nodded grandly.

"In general, this is how it's supposed to go." The blue jewel on the end of his sceptre was sparkling exaggeratedly.

"Do you have a problem?" the Boss asked.

"Sort of."

"What is it?"

"I'm not sure," I answered. It was the truth.

"If that's the case, you should do another replay."

The breeze from the windmill hit me, blowing into my eyes, my head, my belly, smearing me with the elements of the night. The spots on my body hit by the night gleamed black for a while, and then returned to their normal colour.

I did as he suggested, and carried out a replay. Any number of times I brought the girl back to life, and any number of times the result was the same.

"You just don't give up, do you?" I said, as the girl flashed her knife at me for the umpteenth time.

The girl hung her head sadly.

"It's because I'm always new. It's always the first time for me," she said, hanging her head so low her slender neck looked as if it would snap.

I took pity on her, and for the first time kissed her of my own accord. The girl, drained of strength, responded to my kiss. I felt even sorrier for her then, and put some passion into it. And that was when a touch of my old feeling for her came back.

"You're the last replay I'll do," I said, hugging her a little more tightly.

This is how it's supposed to go, I thought, more or less resignedly. I held the girl tight.

The night pressing around our bodies was showing slight signs of change, like cream on the point of thickening. The girl was still weak and lifeless.

"I won't allow it!" the girl suddenly said, in a voice that seemed to come up from the depths of the earth.

Making a petulant sound, she pulled herself sharply away. I found myself on my hands and knees.

"Goodbye!" The girl cut off a bit of my flesh, as she had done before, and went away looking very pleased.

With sadness, I presented myself before the Boss.

"Is this how it's supposed to go?" I asked for a second time.

The Boss answered with an unperturbed air:

"Well, yes—in general, I'd say it is."

I withdrew, despondent, and conducted my final replay. Carrying the girl I had recreated in my arms, carefully, like a treasured possession, I made my way into the night. I kept going, into its very depths, as far away from the Boss as I could.

I nodded off, holding the girl's hand in mine. I slept lightly, though I longed to sleep deeply, and for a while not to wake up at all.

11 HILL DIGGERS

The creature was sitting on a velvet cloth decorated with green and reddish-brown tassels. The cloth had been spread on top of a mound that was five metres high and made of compacted dried branches and leaves with some soft earth mixed in. One knee up, arms outstretched, palms turned upwards, the creature sat in an expectant pose. The base of the mound was quite wide, and all the way up its slopes steam rose in loose drifts, together with the stench of fermentation. Sometimes the steam was thin, and sometimes it was thick. It wound and curled about the creature's limbs, like mist. The creature sat unperturbed.

Waak, waak.

The birds squawked. In a cluster around the base of the mound, they kept up an endless screeching. They looked rather like pheasants, and they squawked and they screeched, stretching out their necks, at times as if to menace the creature, at times as if to petition him. He, however, made not a move in response to their clamour. He was still as a statue, one knee up, palms turned upwards. His eyes, which, depending on the angle, were either a shiny purple or a subdued, ashen grey, remained fixed on one corner of the heavens. There, nothing twinkled: the fixed stars and dwarf stars and the nebulae that filled the rest of the sky were nowhere to be seen, and the heavens were uniformly black, as if blotted out by a cloth.

A bird, squawking, flew to the top of the mound, loudly flapping its wings, and proceeded to peck at the creature. The creature still did not change his pose, keeping his one knee up and palms turned upwards. Blood flowed in trickles from where the bird had pecked most deeply. Another bird, and then another, flew to the top of the mound and pecked at him—and suddenly all the birds flew to the top of the mound, squawking, screeching, flapping their wings violently, and pecking at the creature, producing yet more trickles of blood, which turned into streams of blood that flowed down the body of the creature onto the velvet cloth, leaving blackish-red streaks.

In a great mob, the birds pecked at his arms, ankles, chin, temples, neck, stomach.

The creature started very slowly to keel over, but even so he maintained his original pose, one knee up, palms turned upwards. The surface of his skin was riddled with the holes gouged out by the birds. Deep and black, the holes threatened to take his body over completely.

One bird started attacking his eyes.

Out came the left eye. The creature stared even more determinedly at the heavens with his right eye. Teetering unsteadily in the breeze created by the flapping of the birds' wings, he glared at the sky.

Another bird attacked his right eye, and still the creature glared up at the heavens. By now most of his body was a gaping hole, and it was no longer even possible to tell whether his knee was up, or his palms turned upwards. The vestiges of whatever had been there before remained on the velvet cloth, staring up at the heavens.

Waak, waak.

One last peck, and the body was gone completely. Bereft of the body's weight, the velvet cloth was tossed aside with the beating of the birds' wings. The mound was now the birds' mound: and at the very top, where the odour of fermentation was rising from, dozens of eggs that had been covered by the velvet cloth were exposed. The birds sent up a chorus of joyful squawks and screeches.

Meanwhile, the night moved on, the shadows deepened, and midnight approached, the birds oblivious.

The presence of that creature-that-was-no-longer spread everywhere, filling the space between earth and sky. And the night, enveloped by that presence, reached its deepest and darkest state of being, the darkness a kind of truth in itself.

12 BLACK HOLE

I awoke to the sound of something bursting. The girl who was supposed to be sleeping close to me was nowhere to be seen. I lifted myself up, drowsily, and looked around: the girl was sitting in the crotch of a tree, staring into the distance.

"What can you see?" I asked.

The girl beckoned to me, and pointed. "Look."

I looked in the direction she was pointing and saw a huge firework going up into the sky.

The flaming ball shot up, higher and higher, and then exploded, sending a burst of tiny points of red and orange and green light outwards, like rain. Another firework rose, and then another, then another one, and every time, the girl's face lit up in the darkness, tinged red and orange and green.

"Come on," she said.

Climbing down from the tree, she headed towards where the fireworks were bursting, and I followed. Then she started rising rapidly into the air, as if she were ascending a staircase. She quickly rose high into the sky.

"Come on!" she said, stretching her hand out towards me.

I grasped it, and with her hand pulling me up, I took a step, gingerly, and felt steps under my feet. I followed the steps up, and found my whole body rising.

We rose rapidly, until finally we were on a level with the fireworks.

Up close, the fireworks were very hot. The sparks shot out and fell on us, fizzled, and vanished. We were heedless.

"Let's go closer," the girl said, gripping my hand tightly.

I was suddenly afraid. "Let's not," I tried saying.

But the girl wouldn't give up. "We'll be able to get through." She gripped my hand even more tightly.

With her pulling me forcibly, we charged right in.

"Deeper, deeper," she said. So I went in deeper. I couldn't stand to—I hated to. But nevertheless I went in deeper. One place after another on my body caught fire, and I became engulfed in flames. It was hot, searingly hot.

I got burnt. The girl got burnt too. The fire consumed us so completely that not even our bones were left.

"Why do you do such things?" I asked, angrily.

The girl was silent.

"You can't be happy unless you have everything your own way, can you?" I said, my voice growing shrill.

But the girl said nothing.

"I've had enough," I said. And I left her.

I had no idea where I was going, but I stormed off. I was determined not to think about her any more. I tried not to think about anything. While I was walking, not thinking about anything, I forgot how to speak.

This wasn't surprising: I had no body. And I had no brain.

I kept walking, on and on and on. Finally I found myself at a place that was darker even than night.

I was immediately sucked inside it, and I couldn't get out. I did have the thought, briefly, that if I'd stayed with the girl, without leaving her, I wouldn't be stuck in this God-awful place. But other than that, I didn't think anything.

After a while, I forgot about the girl. I forgot about everything. Every now and then, I thought I saw a face that resembled mine staring back at me in the darkness, but by now nothing about me remained: no face, no body, nothing. So I couldn't ask myself who it was. I couldn't think about it, and I didn't care.

13 ELEPHANT

Having heard that in the west there was something called the Elephant of Eternity, I ended up going on a quest for it. I wasn't so keen on the quest myself, but as it had been decided that I should go on it, I had no choice. Going alone made me a little nervous, so I asked a few acquaintances if they would come along.

"Well, what would the point of that be?" they asked, and then, while I was struggling for a reply, they all found some excuse or other for why they couldn't accompany me. Cash-flow difficulties ruled it out, or their common-law wife had got pregnant so the timing was bad, or they'd consulted a specialist in divination and been given a verdict of "Disaster Imminent", et cetera, et cetera.

I had no choice but to set out alone.

Heading up a path with watermelon vines overgrowing it, I came out onto a square.

THIS WAY FOR THE ELEPHANT OF ETERNITY was written on an arrow-shaped sign.

I had imagined that the way would be beset with difficulty. This was almost disappointingly easy.

Heading in the direction indicated, I walked for an hour, and then there the elephants were.

They were quite small, and they had roundish ears. There was a whole line of them. Every one of them white. Even seeing them now, at night, they were white.

Which one of them was the Elephant of Eternity, though? I had no idea. So as an experiment, I addressed the one closest to me:

"Are you the Elephant of Eternity?"

He nodded emphatically, and emitted a roar. That special trumpeting roar peculiar to elephants.

This was not necessarily to be believed, and so I asked the same thing of another elephant.

That one nodded, just like the one before, and made

exactly the same trumpeting sound. I asked about ten of the elephants, and got exactly the same response.

Irritated, I made my way up to the front of the line. As I moved forward, the number of elephants increased, and they were more and more intertwined.

Soon, I realized that the sight of the intertwining elephants reminded me of something. It dawned on me that it was a mandala. The elephants intertwined on the left side of the road were arranged like the Diamond Realm Mandala, and the elephants intertwined on the right side of the road were arranged like the Womb Realm Mandala.

I suspected I had been hoodwinked. This irritated me even more, so I decided to go back. But suddenly, from the forests beyond the intertwining lines of elephants, dozens of elephant handlers came scurrying out and accosted me.

"You do know those are mandalas."

"The Diamond Realm and the Womb Realm mandalas, no less. You don't come across them often."

"Please, don't hurry off. Stay."

Each elephant handler was dressed in gold brocade. But their robes were a bit shabby, and here and there the gold threads were frayed.

"If you don't like them, there's always the option of becoming an elephant handler."

"What a great idea."

"You'd enjoy being an elephant handler."

And with that, they quickly started dressing me in gold brocade. I didn't like this at all, so without a word I ran off.

I ran all the way back to the square with the arrow-shaped sign, and as I was catching my breath, someone I seemed to recognize appeared. She immediately jumped to conclusions.

"So you're running away!"

"But the mandalas were so boring!" I replied.

"Well, I want to see them. Come on. Turn around," she ordered me, imperiously.

I was suspicious, wondering why I had to do what she said, but I obeyed her, despite myself.

"Come on! Quickly! We *must* get a good look at the Womb Realm Mandala," she commanded, even more imperiously.

So I went back to where the elephants were. I found it completely uninteresting, but I gazed thoughtfully, as I'd been told to, at the Womb Realm Mandala, which was on the right. As I gazed, I started to feel drowsy. I'll just have forty winks, I thought, drifting off. I suddenly remembered I should issue an order to someone, quickly. But by then I was fast asleep.

14 ALLERGY

Whenever we were separated, I would long for her. Even when I thought I had forgotten her, she would suddenly pop back into my mind. In fact, whenever there was any reason at all to remember her, I would remember her. So I decided to go back to her.

I made my way back along an endless windswept path, and there the girl was. She was seated on a single chair, which she had placed on a totally bare stretch of land. To my surprise, she was smoking a cigarette.

"Why are you smoking, for goodness' sake?" I asked.

"My body's changed," was her reply.

As an experiment, I tried stroking the girl's hair: several dry strands came away. With each stroke, more strands came away, fluttering down to the ground. It was a pretty sight, so I stroked her hair some more.

"Please stop," she said eventually.

By that time, her hair had got a lot thinner.

The smoke from her cigarette spread in every direction, blown by the wind. The smoke assumed the forms of all sorts of things, which was fascinating to watch. Cats, rats, weasels... They ran off into the darkness once they had been given form. Sometimes a rat would be caught by a cat, and I would hear it squeak, which was spectacular.

"Aren't you dancing?" I asked. The girl got up from her chair, and came and pressed her body against mine. As we held each other and danced, I glanced down, and there, peeping out from the strands of hair at the nape of her neck were what looked like mushrooms. Tiny, red mushrooms with flattened caps.

Horrified, I pushed the girl away from me.

The girl looked at the ground. She didn't say a word. I felt guilty, and pulled her back to me. I put my hands round her shoulders, and we started dancing again.

"They're going to multiply," the girl said, drooping deject-edly. "They scatter their spores once every few hours. They multiply rapidly."

I had blanched visibly, and I knew it; but I didn't stop dancing. I just nodded.

When the yowling of the cats and rats and weasels, which had got quite noisy, finally died down, and our feet grew heavy and tired, I looked again at the nape of the girl's neck, and saw twice as many mushrooms there.

"They *have* multiplied," I said. The girl looked up. Her eyes, which were dark, almost black, like the eyes of a herbivorous animal, were fringed with long eyelashes. Her lips were plump and slightly pink, and the line from her temples down to her chin, with its fine downy hairs, curved in a gentle sweep.

"You have some on your neck, too," she said, in a voice like a whisper.

I put my fingers to the back of my neck, and felt a number of small growths. I scratched one off, and bringing it to my eyes, I saw the beginnings of a tiny mushroom.

"Your body's changed, just like mine," the girl said, sighing.

A feeling of disgust rose in me. I felt nauseated. I wanted to give the girl a good shaking. But I controlled myself.

"It can't be helped," I said, and I quickened our steps.

As we whirled round, dancing, I knew the mushrooms would get bigger. Their mycelial filaments would increase, the small round bumps would get caps, and eventually those caps would pop open and release spores, countless spores, which would flutter down to the ground. Wherever those spores landed, these mushrooms would grow and proliferate.

I could feel my body getting covered by the tiny red mushrooms. Though I'd hated them before, the repugnance gradually gave way to a nostalgic, almost sleepy feeling, and I became quite accustomed to them.

I carried on dancing, twirling faster and faster.

15 KIWIS

Hearing a small shrill voice at my feet, I looked down and realized that the speaker was a kiwi.

"OK, here's your first question." It was that high raspy voice so characteristic of the birds.

"What food is the most efficient at producing longevity in canaries?"

The kiwi was brown in colour, with what looked like black seeds scattered amid its plumage. Crouching down and peering at it closely, I saw they weren't seeds but patches of darker coloration.

"Come on, haven't you worked it out yet? There are three possible answers: the egg of the reticulated python, the call of the stork at night, or soluble glass at molecular weight 126."

Somewhat astonished at this, I remained crouched and totally still.

"Come on, haven't you worked it out yet?" it shrieked. "The correct answer is soluble glass, molecular weight 126! Soluble glass, molecular weight 126!"

I was still getting over my surprise at this line of questioning when another kiwi appeared.

"In the past year, what is the number of victims of non-fatal lightning strikes?" this second kiwi asked. Its voice was somewhat lower than the voice of the first.

"Come on! Haven't you worked it out yet? The correct answer is...," the bird screeched. "...Two billion and fifty million! Two billion and fifty million!" The kiwi repeated the answer over and over again, running around in circles.

The number of kiwis was increasing by the minute. When I looked about me, there were dozens of them, all identical, and each one fired off a question to me in turn.

"What colour was Henri Michaux's favourite bread-making machine?"

"Which one exists most essentially: a bolt on a door, or a hen on a bar?"

"Which corner of a room gets darkest first on a rainy day?"

"On a cloudy day, which will spread farther, the smell of cornflour or the smell of fresh cream?"

"How many layers above the Cambrian layer are the round green stones discarded in the baths of ancient Rome?"

I gave my answers in equally rapid succession.

"Reddish-brown!"

"A hen on a bar!"

"The east-south-east corner!"

"Cornflour!"

"Thirteen!"

At each answer, the kiwis squawked excitedly, the dozens of them running around in little circles together:

"Correct answer!"

"Quite correct!"

"Correct! Yes, quite correct!"

By the time I had answered fifty questions, the kiwis were getting tired, and so was I. We were all of us panting.

"Surely that's enough. Happy now?" the kiwis asked me, wheezing.

"*Me?* It doesn't make any difference to *me*!" I replied.

At this, the kiwis started screeching:

"That's *outrageous*!"

"See? *This* is why nobody likes her."

"It's *this* kind of behaviour that makes you just want to..."

I listened without saying a word, as the kiwis got more and more agitated, coming out with every criticism and insult they could think of.

"Well, if that's how you see it, how about if I just sell off the lot of you to an illegal trader of exotic birds!" I yelled, finally.

They suddenly piped down.

"You don't have to react *quite* so harshly..."

"We didn't mean it like *that*..."

"That's so *heartbreaking*...," some of them muttered.

"I'm *sick* of it! Just *sick and tired* of having to spend my nights being pushed around by creatures like you!" I yelled, even louder.

Every bird fell silent. Without a word, they started pecking at the grasses at their feet, some wandering off into the bushes.

"Well, we didn't mean to hurt you," they said. Turning their small, round rear ends to me, they disappeared.

The scent of flowers drifted over from somewhere. The flowers must have just blossomed a few minutes ago. Their scent had been blown quickly over on a breeze from the west.

As the last of the kiwis called out "Goodbye!" and vanished, the scent of the flowers grew overpowering. The nature of the air was changing: night was on the point of giving way to early dawn.

I waited a few moments, breathing in the scent of the flowers, but the undergrowth was utterly silent.

"Hey, guys!" I tried calling. "I apologize! I think I said too much!"

But no kiwis emerged.

The scent of the flowers remained for a while longer, trailing in the air.

16 FRACTAL

I could hear a dry, rustling sound. It came from deep within the girl's body.

I put my ear to her stomach and listened. It was a low sound that kept the same steady beat, like someone walking over grass, or like a rhythmic clank below the whirr of an astronomical clock.

The girl was breathing deeply and evenly, asleep. A thin film of odourless perspiration had started to moisten the nape of her neck and the space between her breasts. Like water rising in a lake, it gathered in every single hollow of the sleeping girl, and then brimmed over and cascaded: lines of sweat spread out over the girl's body, dripping down onto the earth.

The sweat poured off the girl's body as she lay there on the soft grass.

Drinking in the sweat, the grass on which the girl lay started to grow. The blades of the grass lengthened, the apical buds grew into branches, and the lateral buds rapidly sprouted into leaves. In the twinkling of an eye, the girl's body was surrounded by a dense profusion of foliage.

In addition to growing upwards, the vegetation spread outwards, producing concentric circles around the girl as she lay on the ground. Thousands of leaves of grass sprouted from the ground, each one putting forth bright-green new buds, and growing at incredible speed.

If I listened carefully, I could hear rustling sounds falling like rain around me. It was the sound of branches growing, and leaves unfurling. The sound was fresher and more vital than the one I had heard from within the girl's body.

The vegetation surrounding the girl grew thick and luxurious, eventually becoming a forest. In the deepest part of the forest, the girl continued to sleep. Pressing my ear to her stomach, I could still hear the rustling inside her, echoing the dry rustling falling outside her.

Soon the rustling seemed to be coming from more places: I realized that even though the forest had stopped growing, the rustling was still coming—from all directions around me.

What I was hearing was the sound of footsteps. A whole host of footsteps, coming towards me, crushing the undergrowth on the forest floor.

The footsteps belonged to the inhabitants of the forest, and even though I couldn't see them because all the leaves and branches got in the way, I knew exactly which direction they were heading: I could judge it from the sounds blown towards me by the wind. At first they headed to the west, then they headed south, after that they headed east, and finally they headed north: the inhabitants were continually shifting direction.

The hundreds of footsteps were going round and round in a circle, I realized, making their way closer to the centre of the forest.

As they came closer, other sounds mixed with the footsteps: whispered exchanges of conversation, the clearing of throats, soft laughter, bugle calls. After a while, between the trees, I caught glimpses of the inhabitants. Gaudy feathers and bits of coloured cloth flashed among the trees.

The inhabitants' voices were now clear enough for me to understand distinct words, and the bugle calls and drumming grew ever louder.

Finally, the inhabitants showed themselves.

Each was about one metre in height. They had round faces. They were smiling, wrapped in ornately patterned cloth, and holding either a musical instrument or a long pole. They were barefoot, and chewing energetically. Their mouths were smeared with whatever they were eating. With their round faces, and their mouths smeared with food, the inhabitants walked in a procession around the sleeping girl.

The girl continued sleeping. As if in response to the rustling sound the inhabitants were making with their bare feet, the rustling sound coming from within the girl's body got even louder.

The inhabitants continued filing round the girl, in ever-tightening circles. When they got so close to the girl that it was impossible to reduce the diameter of the circle, they started to go round, again and again, describing a circle whose circumference remained constant.

The shuffling of their feet, their hushed voices, the drums, the bugles and their chewing mixed together in a cacophony, filling the centre of the forest with sound.

High in the sky the morning star twinkled, and below it the inhabitants tirelessly kept up their circular file. Soon I noticed their bodies trembling slightly after each completed circle, and I could see that they were getting smaller and smaller.

And in the twinkling of an eye, they were now no bigger than ants. Even after they had shrunk to the size of ants, the inhabitants were still chatting to each other in hushed voices, blowing their bugles, banging on their drums, and chewing.

After a few more circles, these miniature inhabitants formed a long line, marched straight inside the girl's body, and disappeared.

When the last of the inhabitants had disappeared, I put my ear to the sleeping girl's stomach, and heard, mixed with the rustling sound, the faint sounds of bugles and drums.

17 LION

Dawn was due to arrive soon, we had heard, so a celebratory feast was to be held.

Numerous people whom I knew had been invited to a mansion on the bank of a river. We were all on easy, familiar terms, so the drinking started immediately, without pre-dinner speeches, and we then turned our attention to the lavish spread on the banquet table. I was drawn to the salted bonito viscera and the salted sweetfish entrails, but since no one else seemed to have any interest in them, I contented myself with the root vegetables and grilled fish.

After a bit, the host, who was the owner of the mansion, rose to his feet and, with his chin, made a slight upward movement. Immediately there was a tremendous commotion in the kitchen, and a gaggle of women in aprons and men with crew cuts came running out. Leaping over the table, they sprinted into the garden and made their escape. A couple of them were not so athletic, and their feet knocked cups and plates to the floor.

The guests carried on drinking, apparently not giving it a thought. The host sat down again, and started digging into various dishes, including the cod braised in its skin, gluttonously.

After several hours, or so I thought, had passed, I looked at the clock, and realized it was still well before dawn. The sky in the east was completely dark. Perhaps because the kitchen staff had run off, the serving dishes on the table were now bare of food. There was only the bonito viscera and sweetfish entrails, in platters at the centre of the table, completely untouched by anyone's chopsticks.

Suddenly, there was a rumble of sound—*Kin!*—and from the kitchen a huge form emerged and passed over the table. It had no corporeality: it was just a shadow. The shadow roared *Kin!* and then drifted from one spot to another in the room.

Every now and then, it hopped onto the lap of the host, and took the host's head in its maw. The host looked as if he had lost his head, as if his body ended at the neck. Regardless, the host went on tipping back the wine, drinking away, his head inside the shadow's enormous mouth.

When it had finished with the host, the shadow then went to each of the guests, and took each of their heads in its mouth. They too became headless, every one of them.

And when the creature released them from its jaws, they were left without any features.

As the host and guests were sitting there, without faces, the shadow became aware of the salted bonito viscera and sweetfish entrails in the centre of the table.

The shadow got onto the table and started to devour the sweetfish entrails, barely chewing them, snapping them down. In the blink of an eye, the mound of entrails was gone. The shadow then started on the bonito viscera. These too disappeared in a matter of seconds.

The shadow now looked around the room. The guests, faceless, were still tossing down their wine. The shadow approached one of the guests, fastened its mouth onto his neck, and began siphoning up the wine in his belly. It did this to all the guests in turn; then it went up to the host and sucked up the wine in him, and finally, coming to me, it took my entire head in its mouth, and sucked up the wine in me.

I thought I would faint from the pleasure.

When it had just about guzzled up everything in me, the shadow started to take on a form. First a gold mane appeared, then a neck, then a body, fluffy shanks, and finally a tail, and alongside those, a beautifully contoured coat of sleek fur. It was a lion.

The lion leapt up onto the table and sprang out into the garden. In the east the sky had begun to take on a faint colour. The lion ran to the sky in the east. It sprinted at full speed, devouring every creature it met in the night.

When not a single creature was left, and the lion had disappeared beyond the eastern sky, the host occupied his throne, and the guests dispersed by twos and threes.

Night was giving way to the first glimmers of dawn.

18 APOPTOSIS

The girl was already showing signs of no longer being a girl.

In a short span of time, her skin had become like paper, her eyes transparent. The ends of her arms and legs had begun to divide into branches; her hair had fallen out.

I gazed at the girl, who continued to change as she lay on the ground.

She was changing into something I didn't recognize at all. I had the feeling I was about to remember something I had forgotten. Because it was something I had forgotten, I had no idea what it might be, but it felt as if I was going to remember it any moment now.

"Darling." I spoke to the girl.

"What?" answered the girl.

"Were you always that kind of thing?"

"Yes, I think I probably was."

The voice replying wasn't the voice of the girl, of course: it was the voice of the thing I didn't recognize. It was high and low at the same time, the kind of voice that might echo inside the hollow of a tree.

I looked at the changing girl, and I started to feel sad, and I cried.

"What's the matter?" asked the thing that had once been a girl.

"You've changed," I replied.

"That's how I'm made. There's nothing I can do about it," the thing said, laughing.

I started to feel even sadder.

"Are you still crying?"

"Yes."

"This is what happens to everyone who is born."

"But I had no idea."

"If you hadn't noticed, it's happening to you as well."

I looked at my arms and legs, and saw that they were now dividing into branches, just like the girl's: they looked like something between trees and nets. The surface of my skin was rough and tattered, and the hair that had fallen from my head lay in clumps on the ground.

I kicked at the clumps of fallen hair, but all that happened was that something down there that had divided into countless branches, like a bamboo broom, swept them together in a pile.

"But why?" I asked, dispirited.

The thing that had once been the girl answered, smiling:

"We've got old."

The moon, which should have sunk long ago, rose steeply in the eastern sky, as it had done at the beginning of the night. As we watched, it travelled across the emptiness, and then sank to the west.

We were still watching when again the moon rose in the eastern sky, but this time it was a little larger than it had been a moment ago. It proceeded to rise and sink again and rise and sink again, with incredible speed, becoming a full moon first, and after that gradually waning.

"Do you think we're like that moon?" I asked.

"Not at all!"

"So we're different?"

"The moon gets to renew itself. We don't."

Several brownish butterflies came flying by. The girl stopped talking, and closed her eyes. The butterflies alighted on her, their wings opening and closing slowly, then flew off.

I felt tired, so I lay down next to the girl. Lying there, I looked up and saw a lion roaring *Kin!* and flying through the sky, as the moon rose and sank over and over again. I listened to the roar of the lion, and I put my lips to the lips of the thing that had once been the girl, and kissed her. Then I grew old, very old, and rotted away.

19 NEWT

"Any minute now, it's going to begin!" someone shouted excitedly—and immediately people gathered in a huge crowd. The lamplighter was making his rounds, extinguishing the lamps with his long pole, pushing against a stream of people going the other way.

The forest had been cut down, and the rivers filled in. The hills had been scraped flat, and valleys levelled. When the land reclamation was completed, everyone in the crowd pulled out saws and mallets and chisels and hoes from the folds of their kimonos, and started to build a town, using the trees they had cut down, and the crushed stone they had quarried from the hills.

People were digging holes and sinking pillars into them, others were securing timber trusses for towers, and others were tamping the crushed stone prior to building residences. The sound was deafening.

In a short time, a town came into being. People whistled as they packed away their saws and mallets and chisels and hoes, and sat down and started to brag about the buildings.

The braggadocio continued till the sun was high in the sky. Finally, when they had tired of that, the people unpacked their lunch boxes and gobbled their food down.

One person lay down to take a nap, and soon everyone had flopped down to do the same. When everyone was asleep, the snoring loud, I poked my head above the surface of the water and sniffed the air.

The air smelt metallic. Moving my front legs and hind legs in turn, twisting my body, I dragged myself over the ground. My front legs were really very short, so I could only move slowly. Behind me came numerous other newts, my companions.

When we finally arrived at the centre of the town, we clambered over the faces of the sleeping people, clung to timbers of the towers, and foraged for bits of food left in the lunch boxes. While we occupied ourselves like this—for we could only move very slowly—the day turned into evening. Even when evening came, the people continued to slumber. After taking a nibble or two of their flesh, my companions and I made our way back to the water. The people slept like logs, unconscious of our nibbles.

On my return to the pond, I relieved myself, and licked the water plants. Whenever the mood took me, I laid a few eggs. When silence lay at last over the muddy swamp, we newts fell asleep. We slept deeply, dreaming our dreams, which rose and burst like bubbles many, many times in the space of the night.

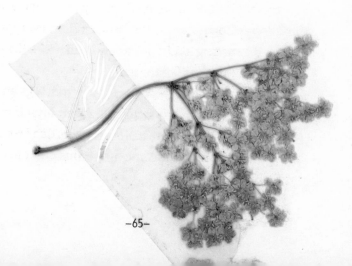

MISSING

LATELY, THINGS just keep going missing. Most recently, my eldest brother—that is, of my two elder brothers, brother no. 1. It's been two weeks now since he disappeared.

As for what he's up to, it's hard to say, but it would seem that he's still at home with us. I just know from the telltale signs: the door to the next room will suddenly rattle, though there's not a breath of wind; chopsticks and rice bowls will be used, inexplicably; shelves that were thick with dust the night before will be found spotlessly clean in the morning. I know it's him.

Since disappearances happen all the time in my family, we got used to it pretty quickly. The only awkward thing in the case of my brother was that arrangements for his marriage were just at the point of being concluded.

The first person in our family to disappear, I've been told, was my great-grandmother. In her case, the word was that she'd been "spirited away", and nothing was seen of her for more than a year. When she returned and explained what happened, her daughter—my grandmother—scribbled down what she said. The account went like this: *It wasn't that I wasn't there I was there right by you You just didn't hear me no matter how loudly I spoke You looked around when I prodded you You reacted to my touch But you didn't see me It was a mystery to me my being invisible to you*

So it would seem that she was in fact right there with her family the whole time. It was just that they couldn't see her. She was able to see everything that was happening to her and to those around her perfectly well.

That transcribed account is the only record the family has of what happened in the case of my great-grandmother's disappearance. Most of the notes that others scribbled down detailing what she'd said got lost over time or used as scratch paper. Probably people were so relieved that she came back after a year that they chose not to enquire further.

But I find it strange that they didn't. True, it was a different age, and people's expectations were different, but for someone to have not been there for a whole year—did they not think that a bit odd?

Anyway, after that, family members started disappearing periodically, and perhaps it all started to feel like less of a worrisome event, but no one seems to have felt the need to look into the reasons. When my brother no. 1 disappeared, the family didn't seem to show much surprise at all.

Well, I suppose as a family we prefer a quiet life. We do have a habit of accepting change in the state of affairs without reading anything too complicated into it—and that goes for me as much as anyone. I did wonder, a lot, about my brother no. 1, in those moments before dawn when time seems to stretch out endlessly, or before falling asleep when dim images rise up before one's eyes. But I could think of no means of getting him to come back.

Brother no. 1's betrothed was a woman named Hiroko, the eldest daughter of a family who lived on the uppermost floor of a block in the housing development next to our own. The Hikari Housing Development is a vast complex, with row upon row of multi-storey apartment blocks that are served by a number of different circular bus routes. When you alight from the bus and walk between the buildings, a strong, constant wind hits you full in the face, whisking the hat off your head and whatever you're holding out of your hands. A notice in large letters at all departure points says: STOW ALL BELONGINGS IN YOUR RUCKSACK. DO NOT WEAR HATS, MUFFLERS, OR EARRINGS. KEEP YOUR CHILDREN NEAR YOUR SIDE AT ALL TIMES. THE RESIDENTS' ASSOCIATION WILL ACCEPT NO FINANCIAL LIABILITY FOR ANY INCIDENTS THAT MAY OCCUR.

It was one of these buses that my brother no. 1, my mother, and my father boarded when they went to apartment 2907 for their first face-to-face meeting with the family of the wife-to-be.

The order of events for this meeting had been decided over the telephone through the long-time matchmaker for the family, Sasajima Ten. A very old woman, Ten has been plying her trade for generations, even before the time of my great-grandmother. Nowadays, since families tend to be smaller, Ten probably gets less chance to demonstrate her abilities, but she still seems to be surprisingly busy, with a huge clientele whom she tells us she has to rush around taking care of. No one in my family has ever seen Ten. She conducts, as I've said, all her business with us by the telephone. Presumably, in the time of my great-grandmother, Ten visited all the families involved at home and sat with them, knees touching, sipping a cup of tea, but on the telephone we never ask her any questions about how she does things, or the way she used to. So nobody really knows.

As Ten had instructed, on a specific day that Ten had chosen, my family made the visit to Hiroko's family, taking the betrothal gifts of dried kelp and cuttlefish, and a chart documenting our family lineage. They were met at the door by Hiroko's grandfather, father, and two younger sisters, who stood in a row spanning the width of the hallway. Hiroko stood behind them, hidden, and it was only after the long exchange of delicate formalities was over that my family could get to see what she looked like. Such rules don't seem to have existed during my grandmother's time—on the contrary, it seems to have been pretty much anything goes, and the same for the time of my mother and father. In any case, on that day, whether at Ten's urging, or because my family was somehow influenced by the way they did things in that neighbourhood, everything in the betrothal ceremony went exactly in accordance with the protocol Ten had laid out.

With the greetings over, Hiroko came forward to receive the gifts, which was indication that she was welcoming my brother, mother, and father into her home. The kelp was immediately placed on the display shelf for precious objects in the alcove, the cuttlefish stowed in the refrigerator, and the family chart put into a frame and hung above the Buddhist family altar. Facing the altar, my brother and mother and father intoned the Buddhist Heart Sutra, while Hiroko's family observed a five-minute silence, and with that the betrothal formalities were complete. The wedding date was scheduled for six months hence.

When my brother no. 1 disappeared, we did not actually tell Hiroko. My brother no. 2 simply took his place. Hiroko and my brother no. 1 had always murmured their sweet nothings to each other over the telephone. The telephone was located in the central room of our apartment, which was not large, and we heard the things brother no. 1 used to say to Hiroko. My brother no. 2 said exactly the same things, in a voice that was indistinguishable from my brother no. 1's, and Hiroko showed no sign of catching on that my brother no. 1 had left the picture. Not surprisingly, it didn't occur to anyone in the family to let her know.

When the telephone call came a few days later from Ten saying it was time for Hiroko and her family to visit our family, we were slightly perplexed. But still no one told Hiroko that my brother no. 1 had disappeared. We didn't tell Ten, either, or ask for her advice. We simply arranged for Hiroko to make her visit, accompanied by her father and grandfather, in one week's time.

Before my brother no. 1 went missing, it was Goshiki.

Goshiki, the name of which is properly written with the Chinese characters 五色, meaning "five colours", is a ceramic jar, a family heirloom that had been passed down through a venerable line that I imagine dates back to well before any living person can remember. It's a great hulk of a jar, and it is claimed that the spirit of one of our forebears inhabits it. The person who started this claim was my grandfather, and at first no one believed him, but he kept saying it and after a while it became an accepted fact that Goshiki was inhabited by a spirit.

Goshiki was so big, it took up nearly half the space of the parlour in our apartment. As children my brothers and I used to try to stand around it with our hands joined, but our arms could never encircle it. It was decorated, as its name implies, with glazes of many colours, and shaped like your typical jar from somewhere in Asia. When my mother put my brother no. 1 to bed, she would say that Goshiki spoke when everyone was fast asleep. My brother no. 1 then started claiming he heard Goshiki speak. *Kuma-nori, kuma-nori* were the words he heard Goshiki speak. Three years later, my brother no. 2 started claiming the same thing. My brother no. 2, however, claimed that Goshiki said not *kuma-nori,* but *kuma-nara.* Then, four years later, Goshiki started speaking to me, saying *kuna-nira.* At that point my mother explained that no one but the three of us had actually ever heard Goshiki say a word. Since Goshiki was now not only inhabited by a spirit but had also started to make utterances, we should perhaps have started referring to it with a little reverence, as Goshiki-*sama,* but we felt more comfortable with plain old "Goshiki" so we continued to refer to it in our old familiar way.

It was the task of the male head of the family to clean and polish Goshiki. Before my father it had been my grandfather, and before him my great-grandfather. Every day Goshiki would be wiped clean, and once a month a special polishing fluid would be used to give it a sheen. In my great-grandfather's day the polishing methods were rather willy-nilly, and people seem to have been happy to leave Goshiki for several months just to gather dust, but as the decades passed the procedure got more formalized and codified.

My brother no. 1 had been next in line to inherit the role of Goshiki-polisher.

It was the day after a once-monthly polishing ritual that Goshiki vanished without a trace.

We were awakened by a shriek from my brother no. 2, who was always the earliest of us all to rise. One after another we ran out of the bedroom where we slept in our hammocks.

My brother no. 2 was in the parlour, his legs planted firmly on the floor, one arm straight up in the air, the other pointing at the empty space.

"Goshiki's gone! Goshiki's gone!" he was shouting, repeatedly. My father and brother no. 1, with open hands, patted the space where Goshiki had been, but no sense of Goshiki's presence was to be found. After half an hour of the family futilely hunting high and low we abandoned the search. Meanwhile, my brother no. 2 was still shouting, "Goshiki's gone! Goshiki's gone!"—sounding like some sort of automated alarm, and finally my mother had to shut him in a closet to muffle the sound.

When my brother no. 1 disappeared, no one yelled out his name or made any concerted effort to look for him.

After that, we saw neither hide nor hair of Goshiki again. But my brothers and I did sometimes hear its voice. In the dead of night when I got up to go and relieve myself, I would hear the refrain *kuna-nira, kuna-nira* waft down from above. When I walked to the end of the road lined with cypresses to go and draw water from the well, I would hear *kuna-nira, kuna-nira* float down from between the branches.

On days when I heard Goshiki speak, something slightly out of the ordinary would always happen. A full moon. Rumblings of thunder. Masses of tiny ants on the walls.

The family etched Goshiki's name in simple katakana into a wooden post in the corner, and before long we started to gather there in the morning, clap our hands to summon Goshiki's spirit, and pray.

■　　■　　■

After Hiroko and my brother no. 2 were married, Hiroko would come to live with us. This meant that we would be a family of six: officially, then, within three months of the wedding, one of us would have to leave. Hiroko's family would be reduced to four, which meant they would, officially, have to take in someone new. Simply balancing out the numbers by making a convenient inter-family swap is not allowed. It's taboo. It would have been out of the question, for example, if Hiroko had married my brother no. 1, for my brother no. 2 to go over to her family and take her place.

I am not certain when this rule of families having to consist of five members came into existence. But it seems to have been in place when my mother's younger brother got married and his wife came to live with the family. This was the reason my mother was required to move out of the family home. Because an inter-family swap was out of the question, my mother had to go to live with a family of complete strangers who resided three streets away. After a five-year stay with them, she married my father, in a match arranged by Ten.

Nevertheless, to follow official procedures so closely and actually to move out like my mother did is now rather unusual. These days people rarely follow rules so literally, and false claims of a family having five members are common. So I doubt that when Hiroko does come to live with us anyone will really have to leave, and Hiroko's family probably won't bother to take in anyone new, either.

I suspect that the rule of a family having five members became a dead letter almost as soon as it was posted. If anything, it's probably true to say that families—like my own and Hiroko's—that have five members are the exception rather than the norm. One can easily encounter families having as many as fourteen people living under one roof, and others consisting of just a single individual.

Certain families also keep pipe foxes for company. These are mythical foxes endowed with magical powers that ascetic mountain priests in olden times kept in bamboo pipes and carried with them on their travels. About twenty years ago, my mother tells me, it was all the rage to keep pipe foxes as pets.

"Twenty years ago," my mother says, sighing, "that was just when I was a newly-wed. My longing to have a pipe fox as a pet was almost unbearable."

Hiroko's family were said to have three pipe foxes, which may be one reason why my mother and my father were so keen to have her as their daughter-in-law.

At that time, my mother tells me, there were advertisements for pipe foxes tacked up all over the block, and it was possible to buy them with a mail-order purchase, cash on delivery. Make an order, and you'd get a pipe fox delivered in a box. The family who lived next door did that, and one day when my mother had returned from shopping and was in the middle of opening her front door the next-door wife came out and told her about it, in some detail. "It's surprisingly well behaved for its size," she said, "it doesn't howl, and you can put it away in a pipe that's only ten-by-two centimetres! When you touch it, it emits sparks, and if you leave it alone, it frolics about by itself. Our pipe fox has done wonders for the happiness of our home life. My husband drew up an ambitious proposal for his work—which is to do with vegetables, you know—and he got it accepted. And the children submitted artwork to the residents' art exhibition, and they won top prizes. But the best thing of all is, pipe foxes have a marvellous smell!"

After chattering on at length about her happy life, the next-door wife went on her way.

"I begged your father to let me send away for a pipe fox," my mother tells me, mournfully, over and over again, "but he never agreed."

None of us children ever had an interest in pipe foxes. Not a single member of my family—neither my mother, nor my father, nor my two brothers, nor I—has ever set eyes on one. When my brother no. 1 went with my mother and father to visit Hiroko's family, no pipe foxes were ever brought out for them to see. And there was no hint at all of any marvellous smell.

As for family structure, the usual combination is a father, a mother, and three children. Sometimes, instead of three children, there'll be a grandmother and two children, sometimes two grandparents and one child. Sometimes the family will be a mother and four children. What's important is that the official number is five. Of course, that is only the official number, and the reality is often different. As I already explained, some families have fourteen members, some families just have a lone individual.

There was once a family a few doors down where there were no grown-ups at all, just five children. Five children: not only officially, but in reality too—clearly the result of overzealous observance of the five-member-family rule. There were two boys and three girls, ranging from first year at primary school to second year of middle school. With no adults to maintain order, this family was noisy. They were continually bashing and banging things, making a commotion till late into the night, returning home, for example, with a large wheelbarrow found somewhere and pushing each other around in it. The family earned the disapproval of the neighbours, and the local health and public-welfare official made any number of visits. Attempts were made at scolding them and coaxing them to be quiet, but with no effect. Somebody then suggested putting the children into care, but no willing foster parents could be found. Meanwhile, the children continued to make a terrible din, and so finally the chairman of the residents' health and welfare association paid the family a visit in person. When he and his assistant set foot inside, the two children of primary-school age bombarded them with flour.

And then, even stranger, the littlest two started tearing about, changing size, expanding and shrinking by turn, rampaging over the floor and the ceiling. The chairman and his assistant grew quite dizzy. Soon, the other children came out and joined in, and a great wind arose, turning into a tornado that whipped through the house, rushing from room to room, picking up the furniture with it. Eventually the chairman of the residents' health and welfare association and his assistant had no option but to make good their escape, barely getting away with their lives. The children hooted with glee, their laughter resounding through the buildings, shaking the factory chimneys and the water towers. The neighbouring families hid behind their doors, trembling, too terrified to set foot outside. And the next morning they found their doors covered with that same white flour. After that, the home of the five-child family was a ruined shell. No one knew where the five had gone. Some people claimed they had ridden on the back of the tornado to some far-off land; others claimed that peals of laughter could still be heard from the apartment at night. But no one ever visited that apartment again.

My brother no. 1 makes himself visible to me from time to time.

Only recently, he appeared to me on the balcony on the east side of the apartment. I was airing the bedding when suddenly there he was, sitting astride the quilt. His face was pale and he looked weak and tired.

"I want more sweet things to eat," he said. After that we made sure always to include jellies and buns stuffed with sweetened red-bean paste in the food that we placed for him on the family altar. This was odd because my brother no. 1 used to be very fond of alcohol. Of course, you do come across people who like to drink and also have a sweet tooth, but my brother never used to eat sweet things. And now, here he was regularly eating sweet things. I guess people must really change character once they lose their visible form.

"Are you bothered about Hiroko?" I asked him when he reappeared. He shook his head, sitting there on the quilt, but he didn't say a word. I wondered if he was jealous because he had to have seen Hiroko and his brother happily exchanging sweet nothings every night. I have no idea whether people who lose visible form feel emotions such as joy or jealousy.

Seeing that Hiroko was soon going to become a member of the family, my father rigged up a new hammock from the ceiling, and my mother hung the quilt out on the balcony to air every day. This was the quilt that my brother no. 1 sat astride, so maybe he was bothered about Hiroko after all.

My brother no. 1's presence would come and go: at times it was intense, at times quite faint. Of everyone in the family, I was the one who was most sensitive to it. Often he would sit on my chest in the middle of the night and I would wake up feeling the pressure of his weight.

"What's the matter?" I would ask him, and he would reply:

"I'm feeling sad."

"Sad in what way?" I would ask.

"I'm sad because I don't have a body. I'm right here, close by you all, but I'm no longer family. That's why I feel sad."

"We're still your family, even though you're no longer with us," I would say. But he would reply:

"Once someone disappears, they can no longer be part of the family."

"What does it feel like, not to be part of the family?" I would ask.

"It feels like you're no longer your real self," he would reply. And then he would vanish, making a noise that sounded as if he was coughing.

I always feel out of sorts when I've had my brother on top of me. Held down and broken. The mood lasts half the day.

Every family has its own customs. It is the custom of Hiroko's family, for example, to gather parsley and mugwort on the day of the spring equinox. The family hangs bunches of the herbs under the eaves and lets the aroma drift through the rooms of the apartment. The bunches of herbs also have the effect of blocking out daylight. Deep inside the dark rooms, Hiroko and her family sit, in the formal kneeling position, inhaling the heady fragrance of parsley and mugwort.

After a few minutes, Hiroko's grandfather will get to his feet, and begin to weave his way on unsteady legs round and round, as if drunk. Then, one after another, every member of the family will do the same thing: her father, Hiroko, her two sisters, all of them will get up and totter their way round the rooms of the apartment. Apparently they carry on doing this for several hours. The only time they broke this custom, observed annually, was the year that Hiroko's mother died, when the day of the funeral coincided with the spring equinox. Her grandfather argued that they should put off the funeral so that their practice of gathering parsley and mugwort could be observed without postponement. But her father insisted, and eventually the family did hold the funeral.

I heard about these events before my brother no. 1 disappeared. As usual, the information was relayed from Hiroko via the telephone in the centre of our apartment. The whole family listened with pricked-up ears, holding their breath as she related the story. That year, Hiroko told my brother no. 1, a number of extremely inauspicious events had occurred in her family because they had failed to observe their usual practice. Hiroko didn't go into any of the details. No doubt they were family secrets. I don't think my brother no. 1's disappearance was caused by anything inauspicious, but maybe my father and mother's not telling Hiroko about it owed to a similar sense of family privacy.

In comparison to Hiroko's family, my family is rather unscripted when it comes to customs: we really only have two. On the third day of the third month, Girls' Day, we gather sprays of subtly coloured flowers from the fields, bring them back to the apartment, arrange them on a tiered display, and contemplate them. And on one evening in the month of September we turn off all the lights in the apartment and gaze up at the moon.

Once Hiroko becomes one of us, we will have to persuade her to give up the formal practice of getting drunk on the smell of parsley and mugwort and to follow our rather unscripted ways.

But it's only these last fifty years that every family has started to have its own particular customs. Before that, there seems to have been little that differed among families at all. When I ask my mother and father about it, they purse their lips and don't say much. Well, maybe I should go and ask someone who's old, someone like Ten, I say. And they reply: *Don't be stupid! Families are just families, that's all there is to it!* Since that's the answer I get as soon as I start to ask, I've had no option but to let the matter go.

It was the day for Hiroko and her father and grandfather to make their return visit.

On a night without moon or stars, Hiroko, her father, and her grandfather arrived at our apartment. Standing in the entrance-way, their arms full of rustling, leafy branches of some pliant tree like the willow, they dinged the bell, and my family greeted them. The three visitors brought neither kelp nor dried cuttlefish, like my family had, only a chart showing Hiroko's family line, which Hiroko's grandfather presented to my father.

When Hiroko's grandfather and my father were done making their introductory statements, everyone present took a breath, and we all shuffled over in a group to the room that holds the god shelf. Facing the eight million gods of heaven and earth who reside there, my father offered up an ancient Shinto prayer, and Hiroko and her father and grandfather joined in, albeit with some embarrassment. There was still no sign of my brother no. 1 even when all the observances were over. We knew this was probably what would happen, but it was extremely awkward nevertheless.

Hiroko's father and my father then discussed one or two matters of finance. When this discussion ended, there didn't seem to be many other topics to talk about, and the adults fell silent. Then my brother no. 2 plucked Hiroko by the sleeve, and invited her to retire to his room. Hiroko went along with his suggestion, making a sign with her eyes to the adults.

Slipping away furtively behind the god shelf, and pressing my ear to the bedroom wall, I found I could hear the sweet nothings they were exchanging. The words continued in an unbroken fashion, now loud, now soft. Peeking in through a crack in the door I saw my brother no. 2 and Hiroko, each sitting in a different corner, one in the west, the other in the east, taking turns uttering endearments to one another. Neither looked directly at the other when they spoke. Each just listened to the other's voice. Hiroko became aware of me standing at the door and beckoned me in, so I went inside and lay down on the floor at her feet.

Once I lay down, I remembered that I used to lie like this next to someone else, long ago. In that memory I could recall someone stroking parts of my belly, my throat, and the palms of my hands.

The person doing this was my brother no. 1. *Nekoma, nekoma*, he would be murmuring, stroking me determinedly. When he did that, I would make a sound in my throat, a continuous, soft, purring sound, and I would slowly turn into something that resembled the creature he was calling. A nekoma is a little creature that is covered with a thick coat of fur on its legs, arms, and back. It has whiskers, and it lives amid the boulders and pillars that form the foundations of a house. At first you might take it to be part of the foundations, but then on closer inspection one day you notice a spot that is a slightly different colour from the rest, and once you are aware of that you see, slowly, a distinct outline that emerges gradually, very gradually, as a nekoma. Finally, it takes on its own form, quite separate from the boulders and pillars, and then it comes out from under the house and starts to walk around inside the house. It walks around soundlessly, and so very few people are aware of its existence, but my brother no. 1's ears were sharp, and he would grasp on to the sound of its steps and call out, *Nekoma! Nekoma!* and the nekoma would immediately go up to him and curl up in a little ball in his lap, looking both half-awake and half-asleep at the same time.

I had never laid eyes on a nekoma, but my brother no. 1 used to tell me so much about them, I found myself involuntarily trying to take the form of a nekoma. I longed so much to curl up in a little ball in my brother no. 1's lap, to be held like a nekoma in his arms. But my brother no. 1 had disappeared from my world, and so all I could do was to lie stretched out at the feet of Hiroko.

"I love you *so* much, I could *die* of my love," I heard Hiroko say to my second elder brother, above me as I lay there.

"*I* love *you*," my brother no. 2 would reply. "With a love that is as deep as a swamp, and as high as a heap of rubble."

"A swamp, you say? What colour of swamp?"

"A dark, muddy, bluish-greenish swamp."

"Well, my love is just as deep, just as deep as that swamp."

"And the love that we both feel will merge together in the murky waters of the swamp, and sink down silently, ever so silently, to the bottom."

"And what will we find, waiting there at the bottom?"

"Why, Hiroko: family, of course."

The two of them repeated their sweet nothings any number of times. But I simply grew sadder and sadder. My brother no. 1 who used to stroke me like a pet had disappeared. I often had a distinct sense of his presence, but Hiroko and my brother no. 2 were now behaving as if he were no longer a part of our lives. And pretty soon that's what he would be—gone from our lives for ever. Perhaps this was what my brother no. 1 meant when he told me he was sad. I try with all my might to become a nekoma, but since the person who used to do the things that made me become one has gone, I find it impossible. I have a physical form, I am still in the family, but I'm sad. And if I am this sad now, what is the point in being here? Perhaps it won't be long before I disappear too.

The marriage between my brother no. 1 and Hiroko was dissolved with a telephone call to Ten, and with that same telephone call Hiroko became engaged to my brother no. 2 since the engagement formalities had already taken place. Both my father and my mother seemed to have forgotten that my brother no. 1 had ever existed. And my brother no. 2 seemed to have forgotten as well. Before I was even aware of it, the hammock in which my brother no. 1 used to sleep was taken down, and we were spending our days as a family of four.

Time passed, and the festival season approached. My father and my mother were taken up with the festival preparations. Every night discussions took place in the conference room of the apartment complex about arrangements for the event: who should be allowed to set up stalls. What kind of pattern should adorn the jackets of the participants. Whether we should drape decorations on the stones. And also how we should combat the insects.

During the festival season we are visited by swarms of insects, and the residents of the apartment complex are always concerned about what steps to take against them. The insects are about as large as a person's thumb. In colour and shape they resemble the rhinoceros beetle, though they're somewhat smaller in size. They fly around making a loud droning sound and sting people. Once someone is stung, the skin swells up with bumps that are the size of a coin, and these bumps then become blisters, which take a long time to heal. The best thing would be if we could spend the whole of the festival indoors and so not risk any contact with the bugs. But we have to go outside: the festival always takes place in the grassy area in the middle of the complex. A festival held indoors wouldn't be a festival.

This year my father and my brother no. 2 were going to act as "living pillars", that is, humans who would lure the insects away from the crowd. The practice involves some-one covering themselves all over with a lotion having a particular sweet smell that bugs find irresistible, so that they will fly straight towards the smell and thus be ensnared. So why not rub the lotion on an inanimate object? Because the insects are not lured simply by a sweet smell: it's got to be a sweet smell smeared on a human being.

On the night of the festival, it was decided that Hiroko would be allowed to come and observe. Ordinarily it would be strictly taboo to go to the apartment block of the family of one's husband-to-be before marriage, but since her husband-to-be was going to be one of the living pillars, she was given special dispensation.

When Hiroko came over, it was discovered that she had covered herself with a thick layer of insect-repellent ointment. "You didn't need to go that far," my mother admonished. "We will have the living pillars, after all. But you're not one of us yet, are you?—so you're not familiar with our ways."

Hiroko blushed, embarrassed. "I'll take care from now on," she said, apologizing. "I'll be one of your household soon, I'll take care not to do anything wrong."

My father and my brother stripped down to their underwear; the sweet smell they had smeared on their bodies permeated the air, and the bugs swarmed round them, buzzing loudly. My father and brother stood stock-still, their faces taut.

In a few seconds their faces and bodies were a crawling mass of insects. "Are they really going to survive that?" Hiroko exclaimed in horror, clearly wanting to throw aside the restraining hands of my mother and the officials of the residents' association and rush to help the human sacrifices. It was difficult to know if my father and brother could hear her. They were covered from head to toe with insects, but they stood bolt-upright and didn't move.

Hiroko started screaming. "Why do you have to do this stupid thing? Why don't the rest of you let yourselves get stung?"

But no one paid her the blindest bit of notice.

"If you want to change things so radically you could always stand for election as a member of the residents' association committee," a committee member said to her.

"All right. As soon as I'm a member of the family, I will!" Hiroko replied, indignant but with resignation. And with that she lost consciousness.

Immediately the insects swarmed over to her, but not one would land on her because of the strong insect-repellent.

My mother and I sighed as we pressed cool towels on her forehead.

With the festival over, my father and my brother no. 2 took to their hammocks and didn't get up for a whole month. Their entire bodies were swollen and covered with blisters: it was a month before the blisters burst and formed scabs. The scabs were on their feet, hands, bellies, eyelids, and ears—whatever patch of skin had been left exposed—and as the scabs hardened they got extremely itchy: in the last week or so, my father and my brother were scratching themselves constantly. There were scabs even inside their ears, which meant that communication during the telephone calls between my brother no. 2 and Hiroko was impossible.

"Can't you do anything about those scabs?" Ten would plead with us on her occasional telephone calls. Hiroko was apparently missing the sweet nothings she exchanged with my brother no. 2 so much that she was growing wan and thin. Her voice did seem to my mother and me—we were now taking her calls—to be growing pitifully weaker. Despite the communication difficulties, Hiroko still made her calls every day at the same time, and attempted to discuss this and that. Hiroko would always end every call in tears.

How is someone who is so sensitive ever going to become one of *us*? my mother and I wondered. It's not something you say out loud, so we didn't express it. But we each knew this was what the other was thinking. I strongly suspected that what had made Hiroko so delicate was her family's custom of breathing in the fragrance of parsley and mugwort. Or maybe it was those pipe fox things they kept over in her family.

On nights when Hiroko seemed particularly disconsolate we went and reported to my brother no. 2 how very sad she was, and he would react with amazement. His heavy, scab-covered eyelids would widen as he stared in surprise.

Why on earth is she letting it get to her so much, he seemed to want to say.

"I think it might be because she loves you," I would reply. And then he would make a face that said:

"Well, I love her too. I want to marry her, don't I? But why does she have to cry about something like this?"

"It's not clear."

"Do you think she's a bit peculiar?"

"No. She comes from a different family, that's all."

When all the scabs fell off my brother no. 2's body and he was able to have a normal conversation on the phone, he put a call through to Hiroko. Hearing his voice, she immediately broke down in tears. The entire family was listening.

"I love you so much!" Hiroko said, sobbing uncontrollably.

"You love me so much it makes you cry?" my brother no. 2 replied, in a bored tone of voice.

"Yes! Yes! I do!" Hiroko replied. And then, bursting into another fit of sobbing, she blew her nose loudly. I was sure that Hiroko's relatives were all ranged around her and listening, in the same way that we were with my brother.

After thinking for a while, my brother no. 2 spoke.

"My love for you," he declared softly, "is wider even than the floor area of the largest apartment in this apartment complex." There was the sound of applause at the other end. At that we on this end started to clap too. The ripples of applause kept on coming, one after another. In the brief pauses between them we could hear Hiroko blowing her nose.

It was the day of the wedding at last. Dressed in bridal robes embroidered with gold thread, Hiroko made the journey over from the Hikari Housing Development. Her family accompanied her. All of them came over in a slow-moving procession, having loaded Hiroko and her furniture onto a truck decked out with banners of white and red, in accordance with instructions given them over the telephone by Ten. Hiroko's sisters and I were the bridal attendants, and Hiroko's grandfather read out the Shinto prayers, and in this manner the wedding ceremony proceeded without a hitch. There were the usual delicacies for a sit-down meal, and everyone ate their fill. When it was over, Hiroko's family expressed their profuse thanks and took their leave. And then off they went, piled onto their festively decorated truck.

Hiroko sat with a distracted air surrounded by our family, still dressed in her kimono embroidered with gold thread.

My brother no. 2 seemed to find the kimono amazing, and constantly pulled at its sleeves or lifted up the hem. Hiroko looked as if she wanted to brush his hands aside, but she didn't and simply sat there looking uneasy. My mother took them to the room where their hammocks were hanging, and closed the door. This was the rite of the first marital night.

As we stacked up the lacquer platters which the sushi had been delivered in and washed up the saké cups, we listened intently, just as we had when they talked on the telephone. But no sound, not even the faintest rustle, came from the room. No vows of love, no screams, no whisperings. My mother opened the doors very slightly, and made a few gestures of encouragement, but neither my brother no. 2 nor Hiroko made any movement in response. Waiting until dead of night, the family entered the room to take to their hammocks. My brother no. 2 and Hiroko were each fast asleep, each in their own hammock, snoring. Hiroko was fully dressed in her gold-embroidered kimono.

Then, suddenly, there was my brother no. 1. Hiroko awoke: in the early hours after the night of the wedding, as she lay there in her gold wedding dress, she was in pain—she was gasping in agony. Something was weighing heavily on her chest. Everyone else rushed out of bed and tried to calm her, stroking her, rubbing her, but her pain continued unabated.

Only I could see my brother no. 1. There he was, sitting astride Hiroko's chest, looking quite unconcerned and kissing her. He looked very happy as he put his lips to hers. Perhaps my brother no. 2 got an inkling of his presence because he was calling out to him, *Nii-san, Nii-san*, and trying now to shake Hiroko. But he couldn't see my brother no. 1, I could tell, because he was addressing his attentions to entirely the wrong spot.

"Hey," I said softly to my brother no. 1, "you're hurting her."

"No, I'm not. She likes what I'm doing," he said. And kissed her again. Hiroko started to get flushed and swollen in the places where he put his lips. Her cheeks, the area under her arms, her breasts, everywhere swelled up, in exactly the same way as the people who'd been stung by the insects. My mother and father and my brother no. 2 paced around the room in a dither.

"Don't you think you should stop?" I asked.

My brother no. 1 replied sadly:

"I'm only doing it because by rights she's my wife."

There was nothing I could say to that.

"Are you still sad?" I asked.

My brother no. 1 didn't answer, but only started to kiss Hiroko more passionately. Hiroko creased her forehead in pain. In a few minutes she fainted, and the tension left her body. In that instant my brother no. 1 vanished from sight.

My brother no. 1 was no longer visible to anyone now, and we all busied ourselves with caring for Hiroko. I found myself feeling a little envious of her. I wanted to be kissed by my brother no. 1 like that too. I wanted to curl up on his lap and have him kiss me like that, passionately.

"I can hear a crane crying," Hiroko started to say. She would say it as she stood next to my mother at the sink polishing our tin cutlery, or as she was massaging my father's stiff shoulders. She would suddenly tilt her head at an angle and interrupt our conversation to come out with it. As soon as she said it, her body would shrink one whole size smaller, with an accompanying throbbing sound: *hyun*.

No one else in the family could hear the sound of the crane—none of us could recognize the cry of a crane in the first place. My father and my mother and my brother no. 2 stared at Hiroko in bewilderment. With her body now appreciably smaller, Hiroko kept mumbling those words as she continued with her tasks—as she polished the cutlery or kneaded my father's shoulders. Since she was now considerably reduced in size, the tin cutlery was far too unwieldy for her, and her tiny hands were quite ineffective for massaging. My brother no. 2 had stopped exchanging love talk with her once the wedding was over. My mother tried whispering to him discreetly that Hiroko had probably started mentioning the crane's cries because she was unhappy about not getting sweet nothings from him. After listening to this with an impatient look on his face, my brother no. 2 made a perfunctory attempt at murmuring into Hiroko's ear, but Hiroko simply listened with a blank look in her eyes. My brother no. 2's sweet nothings didn't have the passion they'd had during their engagement. Hiroko wasn't the only one—the whole family no longer cared to listen.

These days, though I heard no crane, I frequently heard another sound: Goshiki muttering *kuna-nira, kuna-nira*. The words would reach my ears as I walked the frozen paths in the early morning, or the dark roads behind the housing development at dusk. *Goshiki! Goshiki!* I would call, and Goshiki's voice would get a little closer. Every time I heard Goshiki calling, in the exact opposite way to Hiroko, who would shrink when she heard the cry of the crane, I got fatter. As I walked along the frozen paths, Goshiki's voice came pouring into me, and my body got bigger and bigger, swelling up like a bag getting filled with warmth.

Hiroko was diminishing in size by the day; my brother no. 1 hadn't appeared again, and it began to seem that Hiroko was having difficulty fitting in with our family. She became so tiny that she could be held in the palm of a hand. At night when we went to bed we would have to pick her up in our fingers and place her gently in her hammock. And she became completely useless at kitchen tasks. The few times my brother no. 2 tried to talk to her, she would stick her fingers in her ears and tell him: "You're too loud!" All she did was sweep the tatami room from dawn till dusk using a tiny broom. But no matter how energetically she swept, it would be night by the time little Hiroko had finished. At supper, we would find it unbearable to see her listlessly eating her carrot and mustard-cress salad, repeating that sentence, "The crane is crying." In the end my mother decided that it was time to call Ten.

Everyone listened in intently on the conversation.

"Hiroko's shrunk!" my mother said.

All of us heard Ten huff and puff on the other end of the line.

"So she hasn't matched up, then."

"No, she hasn't matched up."

During this conversation, my brother no. 2 was lying in a corner of the room, chiselling a bit of wax. Hiroko was in the tatami room, still her diminutive self, sweeping the floor.

"Well, maybe we should return her," said Ten.

And it was decided that's what we would do.

"I wonder why all my recent marriages have gone bad!" Ten grumbled.

"Is it just the recent ones?" my mother said, her voice curious. Ten huffed and puffed grumpily again.

"I haven't had a single success in all of *ten years*!"

We'd never heard any talk of her record of matchmaking failures before, so this was quite a jolt. Ten carried on huffing and puffing for a while, then reverted to her usual tone.

"How about letting me try with your *girl*?"

By *girl*, of course, she was referring to me. I'd been suspecting this might happen. Ever since I'd started to hear

Goshiki call to me more frequently and my body had started to swell, I had been pretty much resigned to it. Immediately Ten and my mother started discussing how to get me out of the family and off into a new one.

As soon as my mother and Ten had decided on how to settle the matter of Hiroko, they began discussing a suitable family to whom I could go in one month's time. My father and I listened in on the conversation between my mother and Ten, but my brother no. 2 gave his attention completely over to his piece of wax, and all Hiroko did was sweep the tatami room. It almost seemed as if there was no sense of their presence—as if they had disappeared. Even things that have disappeared leave some trace of their presence, but these two were still visible to the eye and yet seemed to have vanished completely. As if to take the place of these two presences that were absent, my brother no. 1 now appeared by my side and started listening in attentively on the conversation between my mother and Ten. My brother no. 1 started kissing me passionately and caressing my breasts, and I began to swell up like a bag filled with water, making soft liquid sounds, and swayed in pleasure from side to side.

Matters with Hiroko were settled with a minimum of fuss. She had now shrunk so much she was as tiny as an aubergine seed, and so we put her into a glass container with a gauze cover to make sure she wouldn't be crushed, and waited for her family to come to retrieve her. Hiroko's family brought back the kelp and the dried cuttlefish that we had taken over to them, and we carefully handed over Hiroko in her glass bottle.

"Do you often have family members who shrink?" my father asked, when it was all nearly over.

"We do—often," Hiroko's grandfather replied, in a confidential tone.

My father and my mother exchanged glances.

"Members of our family *disappear*," my father declared.

Hiroko's grandfather nodded gravely. "Every family has something about it, doesn't it?" he said.

Suddenly my brother no. 1 made an appearance. He was intoning a prayer in the centre of the room. My brother no. 2 was as weak and lifeless as he had been since Hiroko started to shrink. He was still chiselling his pieces of wax.

"Do I hear something?" said Hiroko's grandfather, seeming to sense the presence of my brother no. 1. Goshiki's voice started resounding loudly in my ears. *Kuna-nira, kuna-nira...* Overlaying the tones of the tuneless mumblings coming from my brother no. 1, it drowned out, inexorably, every other sound.

Hiroko's family were just on the point of closing the front door as they left when my mother asked, as if the thought had suddenly struck her:

"Do pipe foxes really have a marvellous smell?"

Hiroko's family looked at my mother in wonder. "Pipe foxes?" Hiroko's grandfather repeated.

"Yes, pipe foxes," my mother replied.

"What on earth are *they*?"

My mother and my father twitched slightly, but recovered in a second.

Once little Hiroko and her family had taken their leave, my brother no. 1 disappeared and Goshiki's mutterings ceased. I asked my mother and father to tell me about pipe foxes. They both looked baffled. "What are you talking about?" my mother replied. My father shook his head adamantly.

"Well, then, can you tell me about my brother no. 1?" I immediately asked.

At this, my mother and my father looked even more mystified.

"You're talking nonsense, girl. Goodness, what a tiring day. I'm all worn out," my mother said, pounding her shoulders. And my father echoed her words.

"I wonder if Hiroko will ever go back to her previous size."

"'Hiroko'—what's *that*?"

"You know—Hiroko, the woman my brother no. 2 married."

"Never heard of her. Have you, Father?"

"No, never."

The wax pieces that my brother no. 2 was carving were spilling out of the room. They had an extremely strong smell. Neither my mother nor my father took any notice of what I was saying, and they went to lie down in their hammocks. I left the house to see if I could catch any sign of Goshiki, and wandered around the park in the middle of the housing development, but no sound reached my ears. Soon it began to seem as if I were wandering around in a dream, and I became uncertain whether my brother no. 1 or Hiroko had even existed. When I returned to the apartment, my mother and my father were sleeping like logs, snoring loudly. My brother no. 2 had disappeared. Only his wax leavings remained.

When I got up the next morning, the excess wax had been swept up, and the number of hammocks reduced to three.

Once again the season has changed. The family has now taken up burning incense. I'm not certain how long this custom of incense appreciation has existed in my family. I have the feeling that before we did this we did something else, but I can't recall what it was. Sitting squeezed between my mother and my father, I take deep sniffs of the warm, soothing aromas.

I am now swollen, tight and fat like an enormous tube. I began to bulge in the last season, but this season there's no hiding it—I'm huge. My mother and my father lavish me with care, keeping me well fed, if only to make me swell up even more. The apartment feels a lot roomier now than it once did, and maybe that's why they're trying to make me get bigger. Some days I can clearly recall my two missing brothers, but other days I wonder: was I just imagining them from the very start? The incense smells like sandalwood, and when I listen to its fragrance Goshiki's voice floats into my ears. Goshiki's voice—the one thing I can be certain is real. With Goshiki's words ringing in my ears, *kuna-nira, kuna-nira, kuna-nira,* I put a call through to my husband-to-be. I have only met this person once, at our betrothal ceremony, and to me he looked identical to my brother no. 1, but since I don't recall what that brother looks like, that doesn't make much sense. Looking at old photos doesn't help either. I seem to remember in real life my brother no. 1 had much more heft—in the photos he looks flat. But the voice of my husband-to-be on the telephone is sweet and low, and that's probably the thing that matters.

When I leave here and go to join the family of my husband-to-be, will I undergo a similar kind of transformation as Hiroko's? Will I too just disappear, even now that my body is all big and swollen? My brother no. 2 claimed that if you sank to the bottom of the deep swamp of love, you'd find family waiting there. I have yet to get any visits from my brother no. 2. When my brother no. 1 makes his visits, he lets me know that he cares. With a huge effort, he pushes my big blob of a body over on its side and then kisses me all over, gently but passionately, like he did that time to Hiroko, and strokes and pats my hair. I long to curl up in a little nekoma ball with my head in his lap, like I used to, but I don't think he could take it, I am so big and swollen. And anyway, he's not here, he's not physically around, so it's impossible. My father intones sutras every day; my mother selects different incenses to burn, and I continue to swell, spending my time simply waiting for visits from my brother no. 1. Goshiki's voice sounds continually, insistently, in my ears, and every day we gather before the wooden post and clap to summon its spirit and pray.

A SNAKE STEPPED ON

ON MY way to Midori Park through a thicket I stepped on a snake.

Once you cut through Midori Park, if you go up and over the hill, then carry straight on through a maze of narrow alleys lined with little shops, you'll come to my place of work: a Buddhist prayer-bead shop, the Kanakana-Dō. My previous job was as a science teacher at a girls' school. I was not a good teacher—I wasn't cut out for it—and after trying for four years to stick with it I quit. I survived for a while on unemployment insurance payments, and then I got this job at the Kanakana-Dō.

At the Kanakana-Dō, I work as the "help". Mr Kosuga, the owner, takes care of the stock, and the orders and deliveries of the prayer beads, and assists the Buddhist priests who come into the store, while Mrs Kosuga threads the beads into rosaries and bracelets. My job—if I can call it that—is simply to sit in the shop and "help" in small tasks.

I realized the snake was there only after I'd stepped on

it. It seemed languid, maybe because it was autumn. Surely a snake would know to hurry to get out of the way.

Under my foot, the snake felt so soft. So porous and borderless and infinite.

"You know, once you've stepped on me, it's all over," the snake said, after a few moments.

Its body started slowly to disappear, and then it was gone. Something indefinable, like smoke, or a fine mist, hung for a few seconds in the space where it had been. I heard it repeat:

"It's all over."

I looked again, and saw a human being.

"Well, you stepped on me," the human being announced, "so now I don't have a choice."

And with that, the snake-turned-human being walked briskly off, in what seemed to be the direction of my apartment. As far as I could tell, she was a woman in her early fifties.

I arrived at the Kanakana-Dō just as Mr Kosuga was raising the shutter. Mrs Kosuga—or Nishiko, as she said I could call her—was in the back of the shop, grinding beans for coffee.

"I'm driving to Kōfu today. Do you want to come along with me, Miss Sanada?" Mr Kosuga asked.

I occasionally accompanied him in the van on his deliveries, but only to places nearby. Kōfu. That was going to be miles.

In recent days Nishiko had been threading dozens and dozens of the prayer beads for the followers of the Pure Land sect. Yesterday we had put the two hundred rosaries and bracelets she had finally finished into boxes, and packaged them up. Today, it appeared, we'd be delivering them to Ganshinji Temple.

"After we drop the beads off, we could take a detour and go on to Isawa hot springs," said Mr Kosuga. He just came out with this. And then, immediately, this: "Why not come too, Nishiko? Take a little break from the shop..."

Nishiko smiled, and didn't reply.

Although over sixty, Nishiko looked younger, her hair black with only a few strands of white—and in fact she looked considerably younger than her husband, despite being, I'd been told, eight years older than he was. A few weeks after they hired me, I learnt that she had once been the wife of the young master of a long-standing prayer-bead shop in Kyoto, and Mr Kosuga had been the live-in apprentice. Watching her toiling ceaselessly noon and night— threading prayer beads, keeping the shop running—while her husband hardly came in at all, preferring to fritter away his time on other pursuits, Mr Kosuga fell in love with her, and several years later, on finishing his apprenticeship, he persuaded her to run away with him.

The story of their elopement was common knowledge to most of the customers—mainly Buddhist priests who had been clients for years—and the couple were still the target of teasing remarks because of it.

"Such connubial bliss," the priests would declare dryly.

At this, Mr Kosuga would mutter *namandabu namandabu* under his breath, while Nishiko would say nothing and smile. Despite Nishiko's reputation as one of the most skilled prayer-bead makers in the whole of the Kantō region, the Kanakana-Dō was only limping along. The couple had had to flee all the way up to Tokyo, far away from all previous ties, as a consequence of their past.

"I stepped on a snake," I said to Mr Kosuga, casually. We were in a diner in a motorway service area, on our way back from the temple, drinking iced coffees.

"What?" Mr Kosuga yelped. Then, carefully, he asked, "And... what did the snake do?" He brought a filterless Peace cigarette to his mouth, and slowly started rubbing his forehead and temple, where the hair was receding, with the palm of his hand.

"It got up and walked off."

"Where to?"

"I'm really not sure."

It was late afternoon and the light of the setting sun streamed into the diner. The muffled roar of the traffic outside could be heard intermittently.

The chief priest of Ganshinji Temple, whom we'd delivered the prayer beads to, was a serious collector of antiques, and everywhere in his living quarters was decked with pieces of valuable pottery—Shigaraki, Shino—as well as other wares and antique display shelves. For three hours we were subjected to a long series of stories on the history behind every object. Even during a brief moment when the priest's wife, who seemed in some vague way to look like her husband, brought in trays of soba for lunch, the priest continued to spout forth on how each of the pieces had fallen into his hands. Please, do eat, his wife urged gently, or your soba will go soft. But the stories were flowing so continuously it was difficult to judge the right moment to begin. Mr Kosuga managed, nodding attentively and murmuring "oh" and "ah", to polish off what was on his tray, and I tried my best to do the same, but I couldn't make a dent in mine. Finally, the priest applied himself to his food, a brief respite ensued, and I seized the small cup to dip a few noodles and bring them to my mouth—but the sight of the cup set the priest off again. "Ah, that cup now..." The chopsticks, the dipping cups, the teacups, the lacquer coasters, the low tables on which the coasters lay, even the cloth of the cushion on which I sat—everything had a story.

After listening to a story about an Edo-period criminal who was executed by a beheading followed by a story about a son who built a storehouse for his parents out of filial loyalty followed by a tale about a big man about town who was elected mayor followed by a story of a wealthy patron of a sumo-wrestler stable who fell on hard times and couldn't afford even to live in a hovel built on the ground followed by a tale about an ill-natured woman who scalded herself followed by a story about a dog who dug up some gold coins in a vegetable patch followed by a tale about a widow who made a fortune by inventing a special cup for people unable to get out of bed... finally, when the priest had seemingly told his fill, Mr Kosuga rose and proceeded serenely out to the van, unloaded the boxes containing the two hundred rosaries and bracelets of prayer beads, brought them in and laid them out in front of the priest, and, when he received the payment, tore off a receipt with care and handed it over. The figures on the receipt had been transcribed in the traditional Chinese numerals. Nishiko wrote out all the shop's formal documents in her impressive calligraphic hand.

"Incidentally," the priest said to Mr Kosuga in a relaxed tone, folding up the receipt, "know any stories about *snakes*?"

At that precise moment, the priest's wife entered the room. It seemed the priest had to get ready to attend a memorial service.

"Lots of snakes are turning up at the temple these days," the priest drawled. "It's all the land reclamation, even out here in the sticks. Seeking refuge, you know."

Right there in front of Mr Kosuga and me, he started to remove the strip of black brocade draped around his neck.

"And *snakes*," he continued, emphatically, "often pretend to be what they're not."

The priest slipped an iridescent blue surplice over his head, put on a gold hat, and, pressing his lips together as if he'd eaten something tart, smirked.

Mr Kosuga took his leave and I followed, bowing our thanks deeply, and the priest's wife came out and bowed farewell as we drove away.

This was what had inspired me to mention my snake story to Mr Kosuga.

"Miss Sanada, do you mind telling me what the snake was like?"

The distant honk of a truck sounded, like the foghorn of a ship. We could have been sitting in a beachfront cafe.

"It was medium-sized. And soft..."

A slightly hapless look crossed Mr Kosuga's face, but he said nothing more and, giving his broad brow one more rub, got up to leave. In the van he switched on the radio. The stock-market report came to an end, and a lesson in Portuguese started, but by then I was feeling quite drowsy, and all thought of the snake left me. When we arrived back at the shop, we were in the middle of an English lesson.

I returned to my apartment, cutting back through Midori Park in the dark, to find everything tidied and put away. An unfamiliar woman in her early fifties was sitting in the middle of the carpet in the room.

It was the snake, I saw immediately, but I didn't let on that I knew.

"Welcome home," the woman said to me, as if I wasn't expected to register any surprise.

"Thank you," I replied.

The woman got to her feet and went to the stove in the small galley kitchen. She lifted the lid off a saucepan and a delicious aroma wafted out.

"Hiwako, dear, I've prepared a favourite of yours. *Tsukune* dumplings in broth," she said. She bustled about the kitchen and wiped the table with a damp cloth.

I watched as she, clearly clued up on which utensils I use and which are reserved for guests, set the table, placing chopsticks alongside rice bowls, not needing to ask which end of the table I prefer. She was acting like someone who'd lived here for years. In a matter of minutes, dinner was laid out: the dumplings, with green beans in the broth, and plates of *okara* and *sashimi*. She brought out two glasses, and opened a bottle of beer.

"Let's have a drink. Why not, once in a while?"

She sat herself down in the chair next to me.

At her prompting, I raised my glass, took a sip, and, finding myself suddenly very thirsty, drained it to the last drop. I waited to see if she'd fill it up again, but she didn't. Did she know I don't like it when people try to pour for me?

"Aah, that tastes good!" the woman exclaimed as she finished her glass and proceeded to refill it. Seeing this, I refilled mine, and just like that, the bottle was empty.

"There are another two bottles chilling," she said, transferring some dumplings to her bowl with her chopsticks. She started tucking into them.

With uneasiness, I did the same—since they did look rather delicious. The slightest squeeze of the chopsticks made the dumplings ooze with juice, so I popped a whole one straight into my mouth. The taste was just like one of my own. After polishing off another dumpling, I drank some beer, then ate some beans, and then had another gulp of the beer. But I couldn't bring myself to touch the *sashimi*. The thought of raw fish prepared by a snake was simply too creepy to take.

The woman quickly worked her way through the *sashimi*, swabbing each slice with wasabi and soy sauce.

"You're home late today," she observed.

"We drove to Kōfu."

I hadn't meant to engage. My defences must have been down because of the drink. Then, immediately, "What *are* you?" I asked.

"Ah. I'm your mother, Hiwako, dear," she said.

"Huh?"

The woman had said she was my mother as if it was the most natural thing in the world, and now, going to the refrigerator, she took out a second bottle of beer. She tapped the cap, opened the bottle and filled her glass and mine to the same level, creating thick heads of foam.

My mother was still alive, living in my home town of Shizuoka. Likewise my father. I had two younger brothers. One brother was enrolled in the local college; the other was still at high school. My mother had a typically Japanese face—she looked a bit like that actress, whose name escapes me, the one who often plays mothers in TV dramas. The woman sitting in front of me, however, had a much more angular, Western face. Her eyelashes were terribly long. She had high cheekbones, and the tiny wrinkles around her mouth and eyes accentuated her rather sharp features.

Suddenly concerned about my mother in Shizuoka, I stood up and picked up the telephone to call home. I couldn't remember the number, and twice dialled it incorrectly. It was like one of those dreams when you're desperately making a phone call but you're all thumbs.

"Hello?" On the third try I got my mother on the other end.

"Hiwako, dear!" she exclaimed, when she realized who was calling.

"Hi."

"What's the matter?"

"Nothing. I wondered... if you're OK."

"Oh, we're fine. And you?"

"I'm OK."

"Is something wrong?"

As I'm not particularly fond of the telephone anyway, I rarely call home, except on the occasional Sunday. My family knows I don't like it, so our conversations last two minutes.

"Dad and everyone doing OK?"

"Not too bad. Same as always, you know. What's the matter?"

"Nothing. I just..." I managed to mumble a few words more, then hung up.

The woman had taken no notice as I talked, and carried on munching food and tossing down her drink.

When I returned to the table, nearly all the food was gone. The woman was sitting, chin in hand, elbow propped on the table, and on the third bottle of beer.

"Hiwako, dear, why did you give up being a teacher?" she asked, sipping her beer, without directing her chopsticks at any of the plates.

With my mother's voice still ringing in my ears, I was wide open to the question. The situation still struck me as weird, but I resigned myself to having to answer.

"I couldn't get into it."

"Into what?"

"Teaching."

"Is that all?"

I didn't reply.

"That's not the real reason, is it?"

"Maybe not."

"What was the real reason?"

The woman drank some more beer, and again refilled her glass. Her arm had come out in goosebumps, and the flesh looked dry and white.

"Maybe I was burnt out."

My students didn't ask all that much of me in the classroom, but more often than not I would get the feeling that they must require something, and I would give them something that turned out not to be what they wanted at all. Then I would get into a muddle about whether *I* had needed to foist it on *them*. That's what burnt me out. The whole thing was a charade.

"Well," the woman announced suddenly, "time to hit the sack," and then, without bothering to clear away any of the dirty dishes, she pressed herself against the wooden post in a corner. How she did it I'll never know, but she managed to flatten herself out completely, wind herself against the surface of the wood, and slither round up to the very top. Once she reached the ceiling, she stopped, and, when I looked at her a second later, she was a snake. Looking just like an image that someone had painted of a snake curled up there, she closed her eyes.

After that, she didn't budge, and nothing I did—calling up at her, even bringing a long stick and giving her a poke with it—had any effect.

The next morning, the snake was still there, in the same spot. I wondered if I wasn't being a bit reckless, but I decided to leave her as she was, and set off to work.

When I arrived, Mr Kosuga was standing outside raising the shutter. I could hear a sound like gunshots in the near distance.

"Bird-scaring rockets," Mr Kosuga said, before I'd even said a thing about the noise. "Do you know about bird-scaring rockets, Miss Sanada?"

"No," I said, and he proceeded to give me an explanation.

Bird-scaring rockets, Mr Kosuga explained, are a kind of device—like guns but without bullets—that produce loud bangs, used by farmers to deter unwanted animal visitors from the rice paddies. They are about eighty centimetres long.

"When we first set up shop, we had wild boars coming out of the forest. We'd hear shots all the time. It was like a full-blown battle raging. Huge bangs going off in the early morning."

He told me, chuckling, that for a time after he and Nishiko arrived in the area, whenever he heard the sound, he'd think her ex-husband had come after them and was taking potshots at him. Brought up in the city, he wasn't used to the noise.

And that was three years after Nishiko had left her Kyoto home, Mr Kosuga added. He left the filterless cigarette in his mouth unlit.

"I assumed it was some sort of practice," I told him.

Mr Kosuga looked puzzled.

"The Self-Defence Forces," I added.

"Ohhh," he mouthed. The cigarette, stuck to his upper lip, made an upward movement in tandem.

"Practice. Training. For battle," he said. "Yes, I see." He went on: "You can't be too careful."

Unsure how I ought to respond, I just looked off to one side slightly.

Mr Kosuga started singing some sort of song, in a nasal tone.

> *You can't be too careful...*
> *Keep hold of the things you love...*
> *Safe in our deposit box...*

The song seemed somehow familiar.

The bird-scaring rockets went off faintly in the distance.

When I went inside the shop, the air still had a chill about it. There was no sign of Nishiko. Every so often she didn't come in, and today was probably one of those days. Her big toe was probably acting up. Nishiko suffered from gout.

I dusted the items on the shelves, and sprinkled water over the pavement in front of the shop, carrying out Nishiko's daily tasks. Then, rather than coffee, since that would be encroaching too much, I made green tea for two, sat down in front of the desk, and with nothing else to do, just sipped my tea.

In a while the telephone started ringing, I had to note down orders, and go back to check what we had in stock— and before I knew it, hours had passed. Mr Kosuga came back from his deliveries, and as we were having our third cup of green tea the sun started to go down. In the hours I spent sitting there, the thought of the snake occasionally flitted through my mind, but whenever I tried to focus on it, the thought dissolved. Just once, during a telephone call from a priest from Shōsenji Temple, one of our long-time customers, I was sure I heard him say the word "snake". But in fact he'd said "simple vestment", slurring some of the syllables.

However, Mr Kosuga brought the topic up as soon as he came back.

"You know that *snake* that you mentioned," he said, checking the items customers had ordered in the ledger. "If it comes to your place, you will send it packing, won't you?"

"What do you mean?"

"That snake that you mentioned."

I looked at him. He looked back. I could see it dawning on him that the snake had already moved in with me.

"So it's too late," he said.

"Yes."

"So you're really sure you can't do anything about it."

He was being a little insistent, it seemed to me, but the next instant he began to croon, in that high little voice, the same ditty he'd been singing that morning.

> *You can't be too careful,*
> *No, you can't be too careful...*

Was he dreaming—engrossed in his own thoughts? Or was he in some sort of a tight spot? With Mr Kosuga, it was always difficult to tell. Maybe it was a bit of both. I was on the point of asking myself whether I'd been stupid to be so heedless, carrying on with my tasks, delaying coming to any decision about what to do with the snake, when it suddenly occurred to me where I'd heard that song. It was at a local festival, coming out of a float sponsored by a credit union near the station. Those lyrics, *You can't be too careful*, set somehow to a musical arrangement, and recorded on a tape that ran on and on, had blared out while the float paraded through the streets. I had sat daydreaming inside the shop, which despite the festival had remained open for business, trying to stop the words of the jingle from entering my brain. But it seemed they had found their way in after all.

"Send it packing."

"You think?"

"If you can, I'd advise, yes."

"But *can* I?"

Mr Kosuga rubbed his brow with the palm of his hand, and didn't reply. He put some banknotes in a linen draw-string bag, and locked up the till. Facing a figure of the Buddha inside one of the glass cases, he muttered *naman-dabu namandabu*, then switched the gas taps to the closed position, and placed a little saucer with a mound of puri-fying salt by the door of the washroom. Finally, he pulled down the shutter and turned off the lights.

"I'm not the wisest man in the world," he said, "but there's no need to take on responsibility for every stray that comes your way."

All very well, I thought. But sometimes you only know what you should take on and what you should not when you don't have the choice. But I didn't say this out loud to Mr Kosuga.

I made my way home, wondering whether the snake would have left or whether she'd still be there. Already the snake was at the centre of my thoughts.

The snake was there. She was in her human form.

"Welcome back, Hiwako, dear," she said.

"Yes, I'm home!" I replied, feeling as if we'd been greeting each other like this for years.

After that, she didn't say anything else. I took a bath and did my laundry. Unwilling to take my clothes off in front of her, I did all my changing inside the bathroom, which was a bit cramped. When I emerged, in pyjamas that were still damp from the steam, the woman immediately brought out a beer.

"Come, let's have a drink," she said.

I was about to refuse, but the sight of the beer made me want to have some. Once I'd had a drink, the dishes of food started to tempt me, and then I had to have another drink. I glanced at the woman. She was looking completely relaxed.

"Hiwako, dear, I wonder if you remember," she began. The area around her eyes had started to flush a deep red colour. "That time you fell out of a tree?"

Fell out of a tree? This was the first I'd heard of it.

"Your little friend Gen from next door ran round yelling, 'Hiwako's mum! Hiwako's had a fall. She's fallen out of a tree!' It gave me such a fright, I almost collapsed!"

She was staring steadily at the air a few inches in front of her face, and her voice got a little loud. "I rushed over, and there you were sitting right underneath it. 'So you're OK,' I said, and you said, 'No, that's the end of me.' That's *so typical* of you, Hiwako dear, to give that kind of an answer."

I had no recollection of any such incident. "Are you sure you haven't mixed me up with someone else?"

"No. How could I be mistaken—your very own mother?"

"My mother is in Shizuoka." This was beginning to annoy me.

The woman went on, regardless: "Yes, that's true, but *I'm also* your mother."

"Don't be ridiculous."

"Hiwako, darling. Trust me. *I know.*"

I felt the hair rise on the back of my neck.

The woman's skin had a glossy, damp sheen. She was looking remarkably like a snake. The thought went through my mind that I had, just this minute, taken on responsibility for this woman, like it or not. I'd had this feeling any number of times, but the specific details had faded from memory.

The woman gazed at me with a doting expression.

"Hiwako, dearest. *I want to take care of you,*" she said, in a cloying voice, and curled herself round into a ball. Then, before I knew it, she'd reverted to being a snake, and slithered up to the ceiling. She became like the image of a snake that someone had painted up there, and she wouldn't be budged no matter how much I prodded and pulled.

I laid out my futon in a corner of the room, as far away as possible from the snake. I didn't expect to be able to sleep, but I dropped off immediately and slept soundly all night.

"Miss Sanada, your voice seems weak today," I heard Nishiko say from behind me as I sat checking sales slips, sipping my tea. I paused to take this in. She had only arrived in the shop a moment before, and we hadn't yet said a word.

Every so often Nishiko would come out with such statements. I'd arrive at work in the morning to be told as soon as she saw me, "You ate too much last night, Miss Sanada, didn't you?" or "Today you're going to feel down in the dumps all day."

But she was often on target. Today my voice was little more than a peep, and my eyes wouldn't open wide.

"Good morning," I said, over my shoulder.

"What did I tell you?" she said, and smiled.

Mr Kosuga entered the shop, making a loud noise. The racket came from the object he carried in his hands. It was covered in a cloth. He put the object up on the glass counter of the case, and removed the cloth. It was a box. There was the sound of something moving around inside it, frantically.

"What's that?" Nishiko asked.

Mr Kosuga put a finger to his lips: "Shh! You know—*that*."

"Oh, *that*."

I pretended to be taken up with the sales slips, and waited for what they would say next, but that was it. The smell of a lit cigarette reached me. I heard Mr Kosuga sigh.

For lunch Nishiko called a local restaurant for delivery of three orders of tempura over rice, and the three of us sat in the little room in the back and had our meal. About once a month, they would treat me to a large deluxe order of *ten-don*, with one extra prawn and an extra-generous heap of pickled aubergine.

Mr Kosuga recounted a story he had learnt from the priest whom he had made a delivery to that morning.

The priest had told him about his son, whom he had been hoping to hand down his priesthood to, but who had, much to his concern, gone off to live in America. The boy was buying up quantities of old clothes, he said, sending them back to Japan, and selling them off at an exorbitant price. Is there really such a demand in Japan, nowadays, for old clothes? Mr Kosuga had enquired. And the priest had assured him that, yes, anything, so long as it was vintage, was a hot ticket for young people, who snapped it all up for huge sums of money.

"So is that the kind of thing young people go for now?" Mr Kosuga asked me.

I had no idea, so I replied, "Who knows?"

Mr Kosuga looked at me in wonderment. "Come to think of it, Miss Sanada," he said, "your fashion isn't exactly typical of the youth of today."

Not quite understanding what kind of people he was referring to with that phrase "the youth of today", I didn't grace this with a reply.

"Times have changed, dear," Nishiko chimed in. "It's not like the old days, when we'd get all dressed up just to stroll round Shijō Kawaramachi in case we ran into someone we knew."

"Mm, maybe," Mr Kosuga replied, crunching on his prawn tempura.

I was silently pondering how things were between the snake and me. With the snake, I never felt that sense of distance, of being separated by a wall, which I felt when I was in conversation with Mr Kosuga and Nishiko. Even when I was with people who might count as "the youth of today", the students I taught when I was a teacher, for example, or my peers and colleagues—or even with my mother, my father, and my brothers—some sort of a wall would be there. Perhaps we only managed to get along because of the wall.

Between the snake and me, though, there was no such wall.

As usual, the tempura over rice sat heavy in my stomach. My voice was weak, and I felt lacking in energy, until evening time.

As I walked through Midori Park, I recalled the story of my great-grandfather. My great-grandfather had been a peasant farmer, with just over an acre of rice paddies and tea bushes. One day he just disappeared. No news came, and my great-grandmother found herself having to fend for a family of five, and to work in the fields. Three years later, in the spring, my great-grandfather came back, and who knows what transpired between him and my great-grandmother, but they took up with each other again as if nothing had happened. Years passed without incident, and long after, when their children had grown up and had children of their own, and my great-grandmother had died, and my great-grandfather was old and frail, he began to tell people what he'd done during the time he'd been away.

Apparently, he had gone off to live with a bird.

The bird had come to my great-grandfather in the form of a woman one autumn day and seduced him, bewitching him with her lovely perfume and delicate hands. So he went off with her, abandoning his family. They lived together for two years somewhere far away, but by the third winter the woman started to treat him coldly.

"It was the bird in her revealing its true nature," my great-grandfather told people. "She started saying things like, 'How am I ever going to lay eggs with a feckless husband like you!' And one day she flew away, with a flutter of her wings, saying, 'I want to build a nest!' And so it was that I came back to my family."

I'd heard this story from my mother when I was a student in middle school, and I remember thinking it was a very odd fable. It didn't seem to have any point to it. Even now I can't really see any moral to be drawn. Was it that frustration inevitably awaited a man who abandoned his family for a beautiful but worthless woman? But my great-grandfather seemed to have enjoyed his life with her too much for that. Perhaps it was that women are utterly strange and unpredictable? But the woman's reaction to my great-grandfather seemed, if anything, rational and understandable. Was it, then, that patriarchal authority in the Meiji period was so strong that a woman could say nothing, even when her husband left her for several years—and that modern women should be sure to assert themselves more? But my great-grandmother had not been exactly submissive to her husband, from what I had heard.

Even if it wasn't a fable, and was absolutely true, what was happening to me was a little different, I decided. Nevertheless, I remembered it the way a person who had once been nearly devoured by a shark might recall a story of someone who was swallowed by a whale.

The dried leaves of Midori Park raced across the ground, blowing about in the wind. It was close to nightfall, but there were lots of children out in the park, playing and yelling. Some on bikes pedalled at breakneck speed on the park promenades. Any number of times a child on a bike came racing up behind me and whizzed by, and my hair would be whipped along in the air stream.

I was conscious of something at the back of my throat, catching, making it difficult to breathe.

"What *are* you?" I demanded, as soon as I set foot inside the apartment. I wouldn't be able to ask once she started plying me with food and drink.

"Your mother, of course! How many times do you want me to say it?" the woman replied. She was absorbed in checking her hair for split ends. Though she normally wore it up, tonight she had let it down. Her hair was very long. When she wore it down, it made her look slightly older.

"I don't understand what you mean."

"You don't understand?"

She opened her mouth wide. I assumed that because she was a snake, her tongue would be forked, so I averted my gaze quickly. But my glimpse of it told me it wasn't forked. It was an ordinary human tongue.

"You're always *playing the innocent*, aren't you, Hiwako, dear. It doesn't impress me."

All right, but I still didn't understand.

"I went for a little walk around here today," she said, changing her tone. "It's a nice area, isn't it?"

"Yes."

"There are too many children, though. Children these days are very badly behaved."

"Do you think so?"

"I saw a goat. In a house belonging to a family by the name of Narita. Did you know they had a goat, Hiwako, dear?"

While we talked, she brought out a bottle of beer, and we ended up having a meal. As I ate and drank, I felt sure she was secretly grinning to herself, laughing at me playing the innocent, and I stole glances at her, over and over. She was smiling, in fact, keeping my glass filled, and then heating up the clear soup on the stove. She looked lovely. I liked her face.

Two weeks had passed since the snake had come to my place. In the shop, we were taking inventory. We did this every spring and autumn. There were three shelves from floor to ceiling arranged with supplies. I had to write down everything that was on these shelves, as well as everything on display, on memos made by Nishiko from scraps of paper clipped together.

"Ten Indian rosewood with agate spacer beads."

"Seven single strands of clear crystal."

"Twelve strands of sandalwood."

I would give the memos to Nishiko, who would transfer the information to the ledger. It was the way they had done it in the old days.

"Do you think we might use a computer, Miss Sanada?" Mr Kosuga would sometimes say. "We don't need one— our turnover is too small," Nishiko would reply, and Mr Kosuga would immediately agree and the subject would be dropped. But he would pick it up again shortly. "Wouldn't using a computer make things easier, Miss Sanada?" The subject never went any further.

At midday, Mr Kosuga returned to the shop with a box again. Something was moving around inside it, frantically, again. Nishiko went to put the box in the storeroom. Half the inventory had been accounted for, and she decided we could do the rest tomorrow.

I set off to buy some cakes to have with our tea. Mr Kosuga came out after me.

"Miss Sanada, let's go to a cafe. Don't bother buying anything today."

As I sat opposite Mr Kosuga in a cafe by the station, I remembered how we had sat like this together before, that time in the motorway service area, on the way back from the temple in Kōfu.

"Is that snake still living with you?" he enquired, as I had expected he would.

"Mmm... sort of."

The snake had settled in comfortably in my place. Maybe I felt grateful now for the way my dinner would be cooked and ready to eat when I got back in the evenings. I had never minded returning at night to a dark apartment, but once you try living with someone, I could see, you do get thoroughly used to it.

Mr Kosuga put talk of my snake aside. "There's something I'd like to tell you."

And this is what he said:

"We have had, as a matter of fact, a snake living with us now for, well, it must be more than twenty years. She seems to have come along with Nishiko—she claims to be her aunt. At first I did everything I could to get rid of her, she was a nuisance, she gave me an unpleasant feeling. But I couldn't, in the end. Somehow, every time I tried, some twist of fate, *something*, would always happen—a relative would suddenly be on the verge of death, things between Nishiko and me would get out of joint, one of us would get an injury. A Shinto priest even came and conducted a purification ceremony, but he said there was no sign of an evil spirit haunting us. So even after we had an exorcism, the snake was still hanging around. After a while, her presence came to seem almost natural, and I managed not to let her bother me. But, recently, she seems close to death, and she can no longer take human form—or if she does, it's only for brief periods. She just lies there, insisting that we cater to her every need. She won't eat anything but freshly killed birds and frogs. Today I went out and bought some birds to feed her. I don't understand Nishiko. 'Just throw her out,' I tell her. But she shakes her head obstinately, and carries on feeding her, happily. This isn't the woman I thought I married. It's scary."

Mr Kosuga rubbed his forehead three times.

"I mean it. It's scary," he said.

What exactly was he referring to? It did sound a little scary, it was true, but whether it was the snake or something in Nishiko that scared him, probably even Mr Kosuga would have found it hard to say. Those words of my snake flashed in my mind. "*You're always playing the innocent, aren't you, Hiwako, dear.*"

At the cafe, Mr Kosuga asked for fluffy pancakes, and I ordered a slice of pear charlotte. We stayed for about an hour, and then returned to the Kanakana-Dō.

The woman tapped me on the shoulder. When I glanced around, she leant forward and rubbed her face against mine. Her cheek was very cold. I felt a sense of completeness—like when you hug a pet, or when you're snug under a covering. The woman wrapped her arms tightly around me. Her arms, too, were quite cold, and I noticed the flesh on her fingertips seemed to have become a little reptilian. But it didn't put me off that she was reverting to her snake form. If anything, it put me at ease. If there had been nothing snakelike about her and she had coiled herself around me in her human form, I would have had much more difficulty. She and I were exactly the same height. We formed a perfect pair, our arms tightly wrapped around each other's body.

As we coiled, she said:

"Hiwako, dear, it's so cosy and comfortable in the snake world…"

I nodded, and she continued:

"Hiwako, dear, wouldn't you like to come over?"

Shaking my head, I gently extracted myself from her embrace.

The snake world didn't hold much appeal for me. Perhaps sensing this, the snake stopped coiling round me, backing off, and sitting in front of me, hugging her knees with her arms.

"Have you ever been betrayed, Hiwako, dear?" she asked, looking up at me seductively.

To be betrayed, you probably first have to be deeply involved. Had I been deeply involved with anything in my life?

I could recall a number of times when I'd been close to people, men, women, sometimes emotionally, sometimes physically, and also a certain period of time when I'd had some sort of conflict with someone, though I couldn't really remember whom, in a place where I had gone in to work every day. But I hadn't ever been deeply involved. Maybe there were times that might have counted as involvement and I was unconsciously trying to forget them. But if I could forget them, they probably didn't mean that much.

"I don't remember."

At this, the woman opened her mouth wide and laughed.

I waited for her to ask something else, but she didn't. Instead, she slithered up to the ceiling. Staring down at me, she called out, "Hiwako, dear! Hiwako, dear!" and reverted to her snake form.

And she kept on calling out: "Hiwako, dear! Hiwako, dear!" That voice of hers would not stop. It reverberated unceasingly in my ears, merging with a swishing sound. The sound of a snake's scales rubbing up against each other. "Hiwako, dear! Hiwako, dear!" *Shu-ru-ru-RUUU, shu-ru-ru-RUU.*

A strange, unearthly sound. Like the sound of a strong wind blowing at night.

Arriving at the shop one morning, I found Nishiko sitting idly gazing into space.

The pavement in front of the shop had been sprinkled with water, the saucers with salt heaped even higher than usual, and the interior thoroughly dusted and cleaned.

Mr Kosuga was nowhere to be seen.

"Good morning," I said.

"Oh, it's you, Miss Sanada." Nishiko's voice was like that of a person who has been adrift at sea and only just made it back to dry land. Something was at her feet. There was a slight sense of a presence.

"I opened up the shop early today," she continued, in the same listless voice.

"What time was that?"

"Oh, I suppose four or so."

Suppressing my surprise, I took a step back, and a bamboo basket beside her on the floor came into view. The presence was inside it.

"Somehow I couldn't sleep. These days it takes ages to get light in the mornings. I got bored lying there in the dark."

So she had come in at four o'clock, opened the shutter, turned on the lights, and then busied herself quietly in the shop? And when she'd got tired of that, she'd just sat there completely motionless, staring out into the darkness?

"Has Mr Kosuga gone out?"

"You tell me. He hasn't come into the shop yet. He's probably still sleeping. Recently, he's been sleeping like a log. All he ever does is sleep. I sometimes wonder whether he'll ever wake up."

Her tone was oddly cold. Whatever was inside the basket stirred.

"Er..." I hesitated.

Nishiko looked up. Her eyes were two shining spots. Narrow slits at first, they gradually widened, protruding, swelling. They were brimming with tears.

"That basket. What's in it?"

Nishiko's eyes were getting bigger and bigger. Now they seemed almost to be bursting, half out of their sockets, the pupils surrounded by white. But in the next instant, all returned to normal.

"That?" she said. "Oh, just a basket."

Once more her eyes started to protrude. Her eyeballs seemed to have taken on a life of their own, and were expanding with speed.

"There's a snake in there, isn't there?"

"Want to look?" The moment she said the word "look" her eyeballs went back to normal.

The atmosphere in the shop was definitely peculiar today. Where on earth was Mr Kosuga? Was he really simply lazing lethargically about... or sleeping like a log?

Nishiko lifted the lid of the basket. Inside was a large blue-black snake, limp as if dead.

I gasped. With that, the snake raised its head and stared at me with shining eyes that resembled Nishiko's.

Nishiko had a slight smile on her face. And then she said this to me:

"That's right, it's a snake. I heard you have one in your place too, Miss Sanada. That's rather unfriendly of you, not to have told me. So, you're a snake person too. I'm sort of relieved to know it. It makes me like you better. You know, I might seem like a mild-mannered woman, but the truth is that, when it comes to people, I have extreme likes and dislikes. I bet that surprises you, doesn't it, Miss Sanada? To you I was simply someone who puts salt in the saucers every day, who threads together the prayer beads, and who many years ago eloped—someone who is basically irrelevant to you. You don't like me particularly, nor dislike me. You just wanted to continue with your happy, humdrum life. But you know, when I take a liking to someone, I take a *strong* liking. Look at my husband: I was once madly in love with him. But he no longer loves me. He thought he liked me, perhaps loved me, changed his mind, changed his mind again, then changed his mind three more times, and now finally he finds he dislikes me. But even amid his feelings of dislike, he has a few patches of attraction. That's what makes him so unwell. That's why all he does is sleep."

As Nishiko talked on in a low voice, the snake glided its way over the edge of the basket, got into her lap, then draped itself over her shoulders.

"What's your snake like, Miss Sanada? I want to know all about it. My own snake, you know—well, she's about to take leave of this world. How will I endure life without her? How can something die, when I love it so much? At one time I wanted to become a snake. I wish now I had taken the chance. My snake did ask me to go over. I'm sure your snake asks you to go over too. Snakes will keep asking you, again and again. But I refused each time. I guess I thought it would be unnatural. Not that I know well what natural is. So my snake must have resigned herself. Eventually, she gave up asking. I've lost track of how long ago that was. If I were asked now, of course I'd say yes. I'm sure it's lovely in the snake world. All warm, with nothing to make you feel different. The kind of place you can relax into, and sleep on and on. Why haven't you gone over, Miss Sanada? It must be so cosy and comfortable…"

Cosy and comfortable. Nishiko's voice reminded me of that of the woman in my apartment. Her voice was utterly different in quality, but they seemed to come from the same source. After a while, I lost track of whether I was in the shop or in my apartment. Of course, in reality I knew where I was and that it was Nishiko, talking away in her tremulous voice, Nishiko, telling me her thoughts. But I longed to swallow what she was saying, swallow it whole. Maybe if I did that, I would be able to go straight over. Over to the snake world, where I could pretend I knew nothing, and just sleep on and on…

A chill ran up my spine as I realized what I was thinking.

Nishiko's eyes were no longer distended. They were back to the shape they were normally. The snake was coiling about her body, droopingly, almost lifelessly. Soon Nishiko stopped talking, and the Kanakana-Dō returned to the way it always was. The snake's scales were jagged and rough.

Speaking of snakes, there's something I've often thought about.

It has to do with being intimate, skin-to-skin, with another person. The first time I bring my body close to another person's, I cannot close my eyes. The person's arms wrap around my body, my hands entwine with theirs, and together we are on the verge of feeling that we're losing our human form. Only, I will be unable to let go of mine. I remain locked within my human body, unable, despite all efforts, to get to *that point*. If I could close my eyes, I would be able to sink into the other person, merge my form with theirs. But my eyes will not close.

All I can do is watch, eyes open, while the other person moves, or resists me, or submits to what I desire.

If, after the first time, we bring our bodies together a number of times, little by little my eyes will droop, the taut outer layer of my skin will start to loosen, and very slowly, it begins to happen. I reach the point when, without having to try, without even having to think about trying, I am almost there.

And then, just when I am on the *cusp*, I see the other person change into a snake, for an instant. The change doesn't happen to me. It happens to the other person— whoever it is that I am skin-to-skin with. It can be a red snake, a blue snake, a grey snake—a snake of any colour.

This is how it always is. Some people I have stopped getting close to at too early a stage for them to turn into snakes. But anybody I have been with for any length of time has turned into a snake once. Why do they make the change, while I don't? Perhaps I do turn into a snake, in fact, while they are having their snake moment. But I remember so vividly the horror I feel when I see the person I am with make their change. Surely, I would never feel like that if I had become a snake myself.

The woman in my apartment takes the form of a snake every night. And with her, I feel no horror. Was she referring to this when she teased me for "playing the innocent"? Was this what she meant when she urged me, making that *shu-ru-ru-RUU* sound, to stop putting on my act and come over and join her in the snake world?

Mr Kosuga was starting to look thin and pale.

One day I glanced at him from behind, opening the doors of the Buddhist family altar. It was as if I was viewing him through a ripple of hot air. I could almost see the rosewood of the door through him.

"Mr Kosuga!" I exclaimed.

"What?" he said, turning round. He looked a bit like a featureless ghost: the colour had quite drained out of his eyes, nose, and lips.

"Is something the matter?" I asked.

Mr Kosuga looked puzzled. And then he asked me in his turn: "Miss Sanada, isn't your colour strangely dark today?"

Moving away from the altar, he came over to me and gave my lower jaw a few strokes with the palm of his hand. He might as well have been petting an animal.

"You've changed, Miss Sanada," he said, stroking my jaw a bit more. "There's a prickliness in the air all around you."

■　　■　　■

On the day Nishiko had been sitting there with her snake, she remained in the shop till evening. Mr Kosuga hadn't made an appearance at all. Not one customer came into the shop, and Nishiko and her snake continued to sit, not making a single movement. I spent the day doing odd tasks, finishing up what was left to take of the inventory, noting the accounts, as Nishiko had instructed me, in an old ledger. No sign of life came from Nishiko or the snake. As the hours passed, they came to seem more and more like some sort of statue.

When closing time came, Nishiko rose, unsteadily, and took an envelope that she'd apparently prepared beforehand out of the bosom of her kimono. "Your bonus," she said, and handed it to me.

I took the envelope, bowed my thanks, and asked whether I should close up the shop. Nishiko nodded absently, as if she didn't care one way or the other. Conscious of their two presences, I locked up, turned off the lights, except for the one in the area where they sat, and prepared to leave. Sitting there in a pool of light, Nishiko and the snake were once again like a statue. This might be the last time I ever see her, I thought as I left.

And she did stop coming into the shop after that.

"How is Nishiko doing these days?" I asked Mr Kosuga.

"Well, a lot better than she was. She still can't walk properly, though. The doctor says she should try to get up, move about. But she says she doesn't want to."

The day after Nishiko and her snake had sat like a statue, Mr Kosuga informed me that Nishiko had suffered an injury. She had been going upstairs with the snake draped around her, when she lost her footing and tumbled down the stairs.

"The snake was crushed to death underneath her," he told me, in a flat tone of voice. "She's now in the garden. I asked Nishiko where she wanted her buried, and she told me somewhere close by."

He rolled his head helplessly a few times, and with a small grunt hoisted a box of prayer beads onto his shoulder. Single-stranded oval bodhi seeds, bound for a nearby temple—they were the last beads Nishiko had threaded. I remembered how with her usual total absorption she had strung them together, her legs tucked under her, on a raised section of the floor.

"I'm wondering whether Nishiko is now going to die," Mr Kosuga said.

Shocked, I looked at him. He was even paler than before, and seemed quite lacking in energy.

"You can't mean that."

"It'd be a terrible loss if she did," Mr Kosuga said, rubbing his forehead in his usual manner.

The smell of incense was suddenly strong, and the air seemed to throb with energy. It was as if several invisible creatures, foxes perhaps, had just dashed through the shop. Mr Kosuga rubbed his forehead again.

"It'd be a terrible loss. I really don't want her to die," he muttered, though to whom I wasn't sure, then adjusted the position of the box, and walked out the door.

That day, left to my own devices, I made tea, ordered myself a deluxe bowl of tempura on rice for lunch, and when I was not attending to customers, I wrote entries in the ledger. From time to time, I thought about my snake.

My entire apartment was charged with the presence of snake. When I say snake, I mean pure snake, not woman.

The woman was nowhere to be seen, but a meal had been prepared and laid out on the table. So, I thought, I'd see no sign of the woman tonight.

I opened a drawer—and scores of little snakes came slithering out from between the notebooks and pens. Gliding up my arms, they reached my neck, and from there they burrowed straight into my ears. I nearly jumped out of my skin. It didn't hurt, exactly, but the instant they'd penetrated my ears, they changed into a liquid and carried on streaming in, deeper and deeper. They were ice-cold. In an effort to keep out the little snakes that hadn't yet got into my ears, I shook my head fiercely. But that only made the snakes that had turned into liquid in my ears become more viscous as they pushed on inwards, into my inner ears.

The viscous fluid filled my semicircular canals. It worked its way through to my auditory ossicles. My ears were now so crammed with snake I could hear nothing, only a distant tiny sound somewhere deep inside as the snakes pushed stickily farther in. The liquid snake brushed against nerves in my ears, and the sensation of being touched there spread outwards, getting into my head. When my head filled with snake, the idea of snake transmitted itself centrifugally to every part of me. My fingertips, my lips, my eyelids, my palms, my feet, my ankles, my calves, my soft belly, my back, the hair on my body—everything that was exposed to the air apprehended snake and broke out in goosebumps. My flesh crept in horror.

Then it passed, all signs of the presence of snake ceased, and I was released. But after five minutes, the sensation of snake took over again. It was as if every few minutes I was breaking out in cyclical malarial fever.

This was not something I wanted to spend time doing.

Rousing the body that was feeling so much discomfort, I made my way towards the dining table. Despite my unusual state, I was hungry, and I crammed the food the woman had prepared down my gullet. Boiled spinach with a tasty ground-sesame seasoning. A sour-sweet vinegar salad of grated carrot and seaweed. Mackerel marinated in sweet miso broth. Simmered yam. A bowl of white rice topped with tiny white fish, minced scallions, and a sprinkling of white sesame seeds. As the food was going down, the soft tissues of my mouth were changing back and forth, now into those of a snake, now into those of a human.

I'd never had so much going on before.

I will not become a snake, I will not. Even as I was saying this to myself, I was devouring the food prepared by a snake, swallowing every last morsel. I worked my jaws onto the food, got it down and swallowed, devoured more of it, got that down too, licked the plates, and then paused and listened for the sounds of all the things that cry in the night. Then I lay down and waited for the next snake onslaught, and then for it to pass, directing my mind away from where I was, forward, forward to a distant horizon, as far away from snake as possible. Stretching out as far as it would go, small and long and thin, my mind tried to feel out any nook or cranny, searching for an exit, but everything was sealed, snake filled every crack, and I was simply thrust back, defeated.

This was uncomfortable in the extreme.

Hiwako, dear, you'd love being a snake. It's so *cosy and comfortable...* The voice rained down on me from all the skies of the world. I was soaking-wet with what it was telling me. The second drawer I opened was packed with a medium-sized snake that was prettily coloured, and when I closed it, hurriedly, the drawer below it sprang open to reveal a gigantic snake, coiled up. Suddenly, there were snakes slithering over my prone body, gliding all over the room, and once they'd tired of that, they got back on top of me, where they proceeded to form shapes of towers and rafts, and lock into puzzles.

Hiwako, de-e-a-r! Hiwako, de-e-a-r! How long are you going to just lie there? Hearing my mother's voice, I sat up immediately and tried to get to my feet, but then I thought it could be the snake trying to ensnare me, and I found myself unable to move. *Don't* become a snake, Hiwako, dear! What's the point! You're your own person! my mother continued. This had the effect of sickening me. Since she was so against it, I felt almost as if I should try it. That's *right*, Hiwako, dear—isn't that what I've been saying? I'm the one who's your mother, and if your mother's a snake, it stands to reason you're a snake too... That was the snake speaking. The snake and my mother started to quarrel with each other. On and on they quarrelled, looming, enormous presences, the snake trying to shrink my mother by hurling at her any snakes in the room—little snakes, wriggling snakes, any snakes within reach—and my mother trying to beat the snake back by hurling incantations, imprecations, and prayers.

I no longer knew where I was, what I was doing, but my body continued intermittently to turn into a snake, regardless, and after a while that physical sensation of snake began gradually to feel quite comfortable. Wondering whether this meant that at some point all of me was going to become snake, I lay there experiencing in equal parts a sense of dread and a sense of calm expectation, the tears falling, as the night continued to deepen.

"Miss Sanada, you seem a bit tired recently," Mr Kosuga remarked, as he ground the beans for morning coffee. Since Nishiko had been bedridden, he had assumed responsibility for this task.

I was indeed extremely sleep-deprived since I now had to deal with the threat of snake onslaughts on a nightly basis. More than once I considered throwing in the towel and just going straight over, but some obstinacy deep inside me refused to let me give in.

"How is Nishiko?" I asked, sipping my coffee.

Mr Kosuga's eyes grew moist.

"You know, she's recovering much quicker than I thought." Despite his relieved tone, he still looked very pale.

Nishiko had emerged from her bed, he explained, at first dragging herself around with her arms, then holding on to furniture like a baby making its first steps. Now she was able to walk slowly without any support.

"You haven't had any other visits?"

"So far, no."

"Does Nishiko really not mind, being without her snake?"

"She doesn't seem too bothered." Mr Kosuga seemed dazed.

Snakes were now coming round to my apartment to pester me, night after night, hanging around in varying numbers. Had Nishiko really escaped from her snake's spell? Had she managed to separate herself once and for all from the snake world?

Mr Kosuga was to make a delivery to Ganshinji Temple in Kōfu. It had been some time since our last visit. He seemed to be stifling yawns all day, and I asked him if he was short of sleep. He admitted he was fatigued, and was worried he might not be able to keep awake during the drive. At his suggestion we closed up shop and went off in the van together.

When we arrived at Ganshinji Temple, the priest eagerly launched into stories about his possessions. Mr Kosuga, sitting there in an uncharacteristically slouched pose, was giving little nods, clearly off in his own world. We both found ourselves so drowsy that several times in the course of the priest's stories one of us dozed off and had to be nudged by the other to stay awake.

"And speaking of *snakes*...," the priest now began.

Suddenly, the topic had shifted, catching both of us unawares.

"There was once a man who took a *snake* for a wife. Well, actually, that man was... me."

The priest observed both of us steadily.

After a moment of silence, he resumed:

"Snake wives make the very best kind of wife. They look after their husbands devotedly, they do housework swiftly and skilfully, and they're also excellent at keeping accounts. And when it comes to certain night-time activities, well, they're perfection itself. They don't have the hot temper you find in so many women, and, best of all, they don't speak much. When you give them their instructions, they listen, looking at you steadily, with those big, crystal-clear eyes. They have something stubborn about them, but not stubborn like human women: human women get stubborn for emotional reasons; snakes are stubborn because that's their nature. But then again, this means they'll keep any promise they make. As for children, you won't get any human children with a snake: you'll only get eggs, and from those eggs, juvenile snakes. But as long as my snake's happy, I have no complaints. I've never liked children anyway."

The priest paused, and clapped his hands together. In a few moments the priest's wife appeared, carrying trays of soba, as on our previous visit. She had her hair bound in a low bun, and she wore a long-sleeved apron over her dark kimono.

"Please start," she said, after she had set the trays in front of us.

But instead of retreating to the kitchen, she sat down where she was.

"I'm now completely used to my snake's ways," the priest said. He turned to his wife: "From what I can tell, though, that's not the case with our guests."

The priest's wife gazed back at him, widening her big eyes. Her eyes were crystal-clear, a bluish-white, and they were wet all over. Eyes that drew you into them.

The priest's wife hesitated. "If I may say something...," she said, in a low, husky voice.

Mr Kosuga, bewildered, stared at her.

"Some snakes take a little more getting used to, sir."

The priest's wife's gaze was fixed on the priest. She did not cast so much as a glance at Mr Kosuga or me.

Then she continued: "I don't think we can say a *thing* about these people's snakes, sweetie pie, unless we've met them face-to-face."

The moment she was done speaking, the antique ceramics and knick-knacks that were lined up on the antique display shelves of the room started to rattle. Nobody said a word. When the cabinet with gold latches that was shaking violently came at last to a standstill, the priest's wife got up and switched on the light. It was not until then that I realized that it was quite dark outside. Although it was early afternoon, black clouds were hanging over the sky.

Still nobody said a word. Suddenly, without a sound, the drawer of the gold-latched cabinet slid open, and from it dozens of little snakes came slithering out. Each glided across the floor to the priest's wife, who picked them up one by one, and deposited them into the bosom of her kimono. A moist, warm breeze was blowing all around the temple. When she'd stowed all the snakes away, the priest's wife slid smoothly over the floor, going first to Mr Kosuga. She wrapped herself around him, and gave his head a lick. Then she came and did the same to me.

"What do you think? Could you learn to like a snake like me?" the priest's wife asked, in a husky voice.

The priest looked on, with an expression of satisfaction.

"Such a question. I wouldn't know how to," Mr Kosuga, turning bright crimson, said in confusion.

"Don't you like me?"

Mr Kosuga, now sweating profusely, managed to reply:

"It's not a question of that. I've never been comfortable with this kind of thing."

"And what about you?" The priest's wife fixed her big eyes on me. "Am I so different from other snakes you know?"

Was she different? I'd never been all that interested in snakes. I still wasn't all that crazy about them. It was just that *she* kept coming at me, insistently begging me to go over to her world. I had no desire to go over. Despite my resistance, though, she didn't stop trying, and came and pestered me again and again. If she kept this up, maybe the day would come when I'd surprise myself and go over to her.

The woman in my apartment was a much fiercer, more demanding creature than this priest's wife, it seemed to me. With the woman in my apartment coiling herself around me, I never felt cool-headed, the way I was feeling with the priest's wife right now. But there was some quality that she and I had in common. For me, the tense, tingling feeling that overtook me when she and I were entwined contained something I found thrilling.

"What about you?" the priest's wife asked me again.

I shook my head from side to side, slowly. The priest and his wife exchanged a look.

The priest's wife's body started to get longer and longer, and after a moment or two she transformed into a snake. The snake glided smoothly over to the priest's lap and then up onto his shoulders, where she proceeded to coil herself around his neck three times. Draped in his snake, the priest launched into yet another story about how one of his possessions had fallen into his hands.

■　　■　　■

I hadn't been sure if I'd ever see Nishiko again, but one day there she was, back in the Kanakana-Dō. Incongruously, she seemed full of pep. "Shall I teach you how to thread prayer beads?" she said to me. "You never know—you might be really good at it." Once again she busied herself around the shop, quietly getting on with her tasks, producing many prayer-bead bracelets. With Nishiko back, the orders for beads, once seemingly in danger of petering out, started to come in again. Mr Kosuga regained a bit of his former colour.

The fine weather continued, and the snake staying at my apartment was once again a woman. As a woman, she was quite ordinary. She had a few snake-ish traces, but she was still much more human than snake. Winter was approaching, so she knitted things and hung the bedding out to air. Any free time she had she seemed to spend out on walks.

One morning, as Nishiko was making coffee, I asked her directly:

"So have you got over your snake now?"

She thought about it a little, then said:

"No. I don't think I'll ever be completely over it."

"Oh."

"If another snake ever appears in my life, this time I really am going to commit and go over."

"Really?"

"Well, I suppose it will be a different snake. I'll have to wait and see."

And that was the only time we referred to it. After that Nishiko set about teaching me the fine technique of threading prayer beads.

Since the last trip to Ganshinji Temple, I'd felt a kind of continual ringing in my head. Not actually ringing—there was no sound; it was like a little nodule, which vibrated, emitting faint signs of its presence. These signs at first didn't arouse any particular concern, but gradually they started to exert pressure. As the pressure built up, the nodule became enlarged and firm.

Every so often the woman paid a visit to the shop. Pressing her face up against the beautifully polished glass in the door, she would peer in at us. The first person to notice her would be Mr Kosuga, and he would studiously pretend to ignore her. A moment later, Nishiko would look up, and she would gaze steadily at the woman. The two of them would look thoughtfully at each other for a few moments. Nishiko's eyes would get narrower, while the woman's eyes would do the opposite, opening wide. As I watched this exchange, I would feel the nodule inside me vibrate insistently.

"Miss Sanada, she's here again," Nishiko would say. "Why not ask her to come in?"

I shook my head, without answering. Twisting the thread, clumsily threading the beads, I concentrated on not looking at the woman outside. The more I tried not to look, the more that nodule vibrated. As she pressed her face hard against the glass, the woman's nose, eyelids, and forehead appeared stretched and flat, making the upper part of her head seem very snakelike. It was uncanny how, whenever she made her visits, we would have no customers in the shop.

If we pretended we didn't notice her, eventually she would go away.

After these visits, we would find fragments that looked like moulted skin on the ground. Nishiko carefully swept it all into a dustpan. While she did that, Mr Kosuga and I got on with tasks in the shop. The last and busiest month of the year was approaching.

"Hiwako, dear, I can't wait any more!" the woman said. She grabbed hold of my legs, forcing me over onto my back. Sitting astride me, she put her fingers round my throat.

"Don't strangle me. You want me to die?" I yelled.

"But I can't wait any more!" she yelled back, a crazed look in her eyes.

She was squeezing, tighter and tighter; my body was becoming flushed. An energy field filled the room. Everything seemed to be shuddering. Thrashing around with my legs, I looked for a weak, vulnerable spot on her to attack. The woman was steadily applying more and more pressure with her fingers. I couldn't get out of her grip.

Saying my name over and over, she squeezed even tighter. Through squinting eyes, I saw the carpet under me flattened, as if wet, and steam was rising from it. The entire room seemed to be boiling.

From the wide-open windows various objects came flying in, hitting the woman as she sat astride me. The woman, hair flying, knocked them aside—shards of metal, crumpled fruit, dead birds... When a blur of confetti in five colours—the five celebratory colours of purple, white, red, yellow, green—blew into the room, the woman momentarily weakened her grip. Quickly I thrust my thumbs between her fingers and started to prise them up, using her hand like a lever. No sooner had I unstuck her fingers than she sprang off and leapt up on the desk.

"*Why* won't you wait?" I shouted.

"Because I know you'll just continue *playing the innocent for ever!*" she yelled, her eyebrows drawn in an expression of pain.

The words seemed to give her the advantage. I drew back, and immediately she lunged straight onto my head and started pummelling it in a circular motion with her feet. The rough drumming sent me into a warm daze. I was expecting her to try getting my neck into some kind of chokehold, but she simply kept pummelling me with her feet.

It started to seem to me that this fight between us had been going on for hundreds of years. She struck, and I sat there and took it.

I was sick of the unending cycle—I wanted it to be over. Those vibrations, which had been steadily increasing in strength, felt as if they might explode out of me.

With a yell of resolve, I started striking the woman with my fists. My fists entered her body smoothly, getting absorbed within her. She seemed infinitely deep, of infinite capacity. The deeper my fists went into her, the more overpowered I was with that sense of a warm daze. I longed just to close my eyes, to fall against her breast, to hear her calling my name. I longed to turn into a snake, to have her coiling around my hips.

I opened my eyes wide, pulled my fists back, and now tried to strike her face with the flat of my hand. But it was the same. No matter how many times I struck, her face remained where it was, white, transparent, undistorted.

"Hiwako, dear, *please* come! Why *won't* you?" she pleaded.

I was at a loss. *I don't know, I don't know,* I replied silently. But I did know. It was just that I was so tired. I mustn't let myself be defeated now. I *was* being defeated, though, so easily. You must want to be defeated. If it's what you want, why make yourself refuse? Was I saying that, or the woman? *It's so unclear, so unclear,* I thought, and suddenly this combat that had lasted for centuries struck me as incredibly stupid and I decided to put a stop to it once and for all.

"There is *no* snake world!" I declared, as firmly as I could manage.

There, I had said it. In a trice I had brought clarity to the whole messy thing I'd let fester for so long. I understood what I had been pretending not to understand. What a ridiculously simple thing to have spent hundreds of years struggling over. Why hadn't I been able to say it before?

"Really?" the woman asked, smiling. "You think it's that simple?" And she set about strangling me again.

I became conscious of a loud zapping sound. The energy that had been generated was filling the room with an electric charge, producing flashes of intensely blue and white light; soon, droplets of water started to fall from the ceiling. The droplets became drops that fell faster and faster, and the room started to fill with water. The water rose from our heels to our knees, from our knees to our hips, and the woman and I continued to thrash around in it. Soon the room became totally submerged in water, and we were still fighting. The entire apartment building became engulfed, and started to drift away, joining the muddy stream that cut though Midori Park heading towards the Kanakana-Dō. But still neither of us would concede.

"Just come over. You'll see that I'm right. You don't know what you're refusing!"

"I'm telling you—it doesn't exist."

"But Hiwako, dear, you should listen to me. I *am* your mother!"

"You are not!"

"Well, let me explain!"

"No."

"How will you understand, if you don't listen?"

"I don't want to understand!"

"See what I mean? Putting on your little act!"

As we yelled, the room and everything in it was being swept away. It was early morning, and the Kanakana-Dō's shutter had been raised. Mr Kosuga was sweeping the pavement in front of the shop. I could see Nishiko sitting at her desk, quietly threading strands of prayer beads. In front of the shop a festival float crammed with flowers and girls in traditional dancing costumes was being pulled merrily along on its way, and from the float came a song, the song of the credit association, playing loudly over the speakers:

> *You can't be too careful.*
> *Keep hold of the things you love...*

The words rose up around the Kanakana-Dō in an endlessly coiling loop of sound, while inside the shop I could see Mr Kosuga and Nishiko, unperturbed, busy with their tasks. Miss Sanada, it's important to practise, to keep on your guard, Mr Kosuga told me, watching me as I floated by, giving me a wink. This isn't "practice", I retorted—and even on your guard, things can still catch you when you're unawares! But Mr Kosuga merely rubbed his head, a filterless cigarette in his mouth, his usual impassive self.

"Hiwako, dear, stop being so stubborn, open your eyes!" the woman was saying.

"*You* should open *your* eyes!"

"Oh, that's so hypocritical."

The woman was squeezing her fingers tighter and tighter. She still had that expression on her face, an indeterminate mixture of pleasure and pain. Well, if she is strangling *me*, I thought, placing my fingers around her neck...

In the flashes of intense blue and white light, everything around became dazzlingly, searingly bright, and surrounded by that brightness, pitting our equal strengths, the woman and I struggled, locked in a battle to throttle each other, as the apartment hurtled away at an unbelievable speed.

PUSHKIN PRESS

Pushkin Press was founded in 1997, and publishes novels, essays, memoirs, children's books—everything from timeless classics to the urgent and contemporary.

Our books represent exciting, high-quality writing from around the world: we publish some of the twentieth century's most widely acclaimed, brilliant authors such as Stefan Zweig, Marcel Aymé, Teffi, Antal Szerb, Gaito Gazdanov and Yasushi Inoue, as well as compelling and award-winning contemporary writers, including Andrés Neuman, Edith Pearlman, Eka Kurniawan and Ayelet Gundar-Goshen.

Pushkin Press publishes the world's best stories, to be read and read again. Here are just some of the titles from our long and varied list. To discover more, visit www.pushkinpress.com.

═══

THE SPECTRE OF ALEXANDER WOLF
GAITO GAZDANOV

'A mesmerising work of literature' Antony Beevor

SUMMER BEFORE THE DARK
VOLKER WEIDERMANN

'For such a slim book to convey with such poignancy the extinction of a generation of "Great Europeans" is a triumph' *Sunday Telegraph*

MESSAGES FROM A LOST WORLD
STEFAN ZWEIG

'At a time of monetary crisis and political disorder... Zweig's celebration of the brotherhood of peoples reminds us that there is another way' *The Nation*

BINOCULAR VISION
EDITH PEARLMAN

'A genius of the short story' Mark Lawson, *Guardian*

IN THE BEGINNING WAS THE SEA

TOMÁS GONZÁLEZ

'Smoothly intriguing narrative, with its touches of sinister, Patricia Highsmith-like menace' *Irish Times*

BEWARE OF PITY

STEFAN ZWEIG

'Zweig's fictional masterpiece' *Guardian*

THE ENCOUNTER

PETRU POPESCU

'A book that suggests new ways of looking at the world and our place within it' *Sunday Telegraph*

WAKE UP, SIR!

JONATHAN AMES

'The novel is extremely funny but it is also sad and poignant, and almost incredibly clever' *Guardian*

THE WORLD OF YESTERDAY

STEFAN ZWEIG

'*The World of Yesterday* is one of the greatest memoirs of the twentieth century, as perfect in its evocation of the world Zweig loved, as it is in its portrayal of how that world was destroyed' David Hare

WAKING LIONS

AYELET GUNDAR-GOSHEN

'A literary thriller that is used as a vehicle to explore big moral issues. I loved everything about it' *Daily Mail*

BONITA AVENUE

PETER BUWALDA

'One wild ride: a swirling helix of a family saga… a new writer as toe-curling as early Roth, as roomy as Franzen and as caustic as Houellebecq' *Sunday Telegraph*

JOURNEY BY MOONLIGHT

ANTAL SZERB

'Just divine… makes you imagine the author has had private access to your own soul' Nicholas Lezard, *Guardian*